TERRY MURPHY

HE RODE WITH QUANTRILL

Complete and Unabridged

LINFORD
Leicester

First published in Great Britain in 1994 by
Robert Hale Limited
London

First Linford Edition
published 1997
by arrangement with
Robert Hale Limited
London

British Library CIP Data

Murphy, Terry, *1962*–
He rode with Quantrill.—Large print ed.—
Linford western library
1. English fiction—20th century
2. Large type books
I. Title
823.9′14 [F]

ISBN 0–7089–5048–5

Published by
F. A. Thorpe (Publishing) Ltd.
Anstey, Leicestershire

Set by Words & Graphics Ltd.
Anstey, Leicestershire
Printed and bound in Great Britain by
T. J. Press (Padstow) Ltd., Padstow, Cornwall

This book is printed on acid-free paper

1

MEL BECHER was a rarity in
a land of boastful men. He
was a quiet guy, almost kind
of shy, so you would never guess that
he had been one of Quantrill's riders.
Yet there was a hardness to him that
showed up at a second look. Though
not much above average height, Becher
was well muscled, and he had that
natural grace that has a man move
like a cat, and lets you know that
when he has to make a move it will
be fast and accurate. He went back a
long way, too, and if he was a talker,
which he sure wasn't, he could tell
of that night in '63 when a skinny,
white-faced kid of sixteen rode straight
up to William Clarke Quantrill, looked
the great guerrilla leader in the eye,
calm as you like, and asked to join
up with his notorious raiders.

That was in Missouri, and that kid and his step-daddy had just been roughed-up by the State militiamen, who had wanted to know where they could find the kid's big brother, who was riding with Quantrill. The elder brother's name was Frank, and that kid was none other than Jesse James.

Though Quantrill liked the guts the kid showed, he wasn't about to take on some youngster who didn't look like he was strong enough to make a long ride, let alone fight at the end of it. But Mel Becher wasn't one to put up with injustice of any kind, and, beside that, he had felt that the kid had something about him. That something was indefinable, being a quality that only a fighting man can recognize in another like him. Anyway, the usually taciturn Becher was about to speak up for the kid, when he was saved the trouble by Bloody Bill Anderson, Quantrill's right-hand man.

"Give the kid a go, Cap'n," Bloody Bill said with that sideways grin of his on his tough face. It is said that he was still grinning later, when he was cut down in a hail of .44 bullets in Orrick, Ray County Missouri. But that was in the future at that time, and Bloody Bill just stood there waiting, like all the others, Becher in particular, to see how Quantrill would react — which was always anybody's guess. He'd gun a man down for this kind of interference, but Bloody Bill was safe enough, as Mel Becher would have been, for Quantrill had a lot of respect for him. Some went so far, when out of his hearing, to opine that Becher was one of the few men he was scared of.

Quantrill gave what Anderson had asked some thought, then said in the studied way he had of dealing with even the most minor problems, being fussy about detail, "I want soldiers, but if you want the kid with us, then he's your responsibility."

Waving a hand that said he accepted that, Bloody Bill gestured for the kid to dismount, and young Jesse James stepped down from his horse into a life in which he would live, and die, by the gun. No one had consulted Frank James as to whether or not he wanted his little brother along, for the James boys weren't nothing to speak of in those days.

Anyway, as it turned out, when Quantrill and his men hit the Federal garrison at Richfield on May 19th that year, it was Becher who took care of the keen but green Jesse James, because Bloody Bill Anderson, as always, got carried away in the heat of battle. The young don't see danger like older folk do, and Jesse, who was on the left flank in the attack, had come riding in, bent over so that his face rested against the neck of his horse, heading straight for an adobe outbuilding, behind which four Federal soldiers had their rifles trained on him — just waiting for the kid to get closer.

Had it not been for Mel Becher that day, the history of the West would have read very different, and a whole

4

lot less interesting. Splitting from the main attack, Becher spurred his horse toward the adobe building, needing to get there before Jesse, as there was so much gunfire any shouted warning would be lost. When the soldiers saw Becher coming and opened fire, the James boy saw what was happening and reined up, his pale face going even whiter as he realized what a close call he'd had.

Not allowing his horse to slacken pace, Becher had ridden past the house, then wheeled in a cloud of dust when he was behind the building, bringing down two of the soldiers with his rifle, before riding behind a protecting wall and dismounting. With Jesse having recovered himself and riding slowly forwards, rifle at the ready, the remaining two soldiers had to watch both in front and behind. The way Becher could move made it impossible for them. They had their elbows on a low wall, rifles trained on Jesse James as Mel Becher stepped round a corner behind them. Both of the Federal men died as his .45 barked just twice.

Jesse didn't say a word when he rode up, first looking down at the four dead soldiers, then to where Becher stood. For a second it seemed that his dust-caked lips were moving, and that he might be about to say thanks. But the youngster stayed quiet, his eyes taking in everything about Mel Becher, like he was either determined to remember him for the favour, or maybe reminding himself that here was one fast gun to avoid in the future. What Jesse was really thinking wouldn't be known to Becher for a number of years, and then it would cause him grief.

They rode on together then, the kid and the man who wasn't no more than six years older than him, until they joined the main attacking force and Jesse moved away to be at Bloody Bill Anderson's side.

The boy fought well that day, and when the garrison commander, Captain

Sessions, had been fatally wounded, and those Federal soldiers still alive either gave themselves up or ran, Quantrill looked right proud to have Jesse James riding close to him as they left the scene of an impressive victory.

After that time, Mel Becher didn't have much to do with Jesse, who hung around with his brother, Frank, and found a good amigo in Cole Younger. This suited Becher right enough, as he wasn't the sort of man to need companions, and he had hardly given Jesse James another thought through a series of attacks like the one along the road to Rocheport in September that same year of '63.

A Quantrill scout had come back to report about ninety Federal militiamen coming their way, and the fifty or so raiders formed up, mounted and eight abreast, across the road the soldiers were approaching on. Giving a rebel's yell, Quantrill's men attacked, Jesse to the fore, and before darkness fell to permit them to withdraw, thirty Federal soldiers had been killed.

Jesse James sure had been bloodied, but shortly afterwards he was going to get a lesson in brutality from Bloody Bill Anderson, in an incident that had Becher decide that, right soon, he would leave Quantrill's raiders.

This was later in that month of September, at a place south-east of Centralia, Missouri, where Quantrill's men came across a stagecoach from Columbia while they were on their way to join Confederate General Price's company. They had searched the passengers to satisfy themselves that they were not Federal sympathisers, Bloody Bill Anderson being in a foul mood because a compadre of his had been captured.

As they were about to leave, a westbound passenger train pulled up. Inside were twenty-three Federal soldiers on leave, heading for home. Pulling them all out, Bloody Bill had selected one man to hold as hostage for his buddy, then slaughtered the remaining twenty-two in cold blood. To put a finishing touch to the atrocity, Bloody Bill set fire to the train, opened up the throttle and sent it careering down the track.

Noticing Jesse James right then, the kid's eyes glowing with excitement, Becher had felt a massive regret, and this feeling increased when Jesse had been among a party of ten men Quantrill had sent out as a kind of diversion for Major Johnson and his troops, who were trying to catch the guerrillas. The ten rode at a safe distance from Johnson's lines; occasionally moving closer to let loose a few shots, then darting away again.

Though he hadn't been there, Becher heard all about the skirmish when the ten rode back unharmed. Major Johnson, brave but foolhardy, had become incensed by the guerrillas, and had come riding out at them, brandishing a Navy dragoon revolver. With the troops deprived of a commander, the main body of Quantrill's raiders had moved in on them, killing sixty, while out at the diversion, Jesse had shot Major Johnson, then had taken his belt and revolver as souvenirs. Recognizing this as the point of no return for the boy, Becher was saddened, but, a few days later, he felt there could be hope when Jesse was wounded in the left side and left arm when the guerrillas were ambushed.

The kid took his injuries very badly, revealing a weaker part of his character by being convinced that he was about to die, and sending a message to his mother to that effect. Watching and listening, Becher made a mental note of this. He had come to know both Quantrill and Bloody Bill Anderson so well that he came close to reading their thoughts. Always anxious to have the measure of any man who might be dangerous behind a gun, he had marked down this flaw in Jesse James for possible future reference, but had no way of appreciating just how vital the information would be to him when several years had passed by.

Despite his fatalistic view of his wounds, Jesse James recovered, and demonstrated his daring in a different way when Quantrill was camped four miles out of Independence. Alerted by giggling among senior members of the group, and the unusual appearance of a smile on the face of Quantrill, Mel Becher was disgusted when he saw a girl mincing her way out of camp, and had learned that it was Jesse in disguise, on his way into town on a reconnaissance mission. He returned to report that he had visited a bordello, where the madam and the girls had bragged that they were very popular with Federal officers.

That night Quantrill and his men concealed themselves in brush not far from the house, and killed twelve bluecoats who had been on their way to seek the company of the girls.

Back at camp, Quantrill and Bloody Bill pounded Jesse on the back for a job well done, and the kid grinned happily at the praise, but the covertly watching Becher had been sickened at the lengths the James boy had gone to — lengths which no real man would even contemplate, and he could sense that Frank James was embarrassed by the episode.

A few days later, on 13th August 1864, while Quantrill and his sixty-five men were encamped at Flat Rock, near the Grand River, there was no time to play games, no opportunity to dress up, as a woman or otherwise, when 300 Federal soldiers, backed by some 150 Jayhawkers or Red Legs (wandering bands of armed men) launched a surprise attack.

The guerrillas were scattered in confusion, and Becher was mounting his horse and about to ride away when he saw Jesse James, who had been running towards his mount, stop in his tracks, lift up in the air as he was hit, and spin round before slumping heavily to the ground. Riding away, Mel Becher had become conscience-stricken. With lead whistling around him, he had wheeled his horse about and ridden to where he had seen the boy go down.

Swinging down from his horse, he had shot a Federal man who was raising a musket at him, and used his .45 to club a nearer soldier senseless, before quickly kneeling beside Jesse James.

Blood had darkened the boy's coat at the chest. He lay on his back, eyes not quite closed. Looking at his face, Becher knew the worst as he saw thick blood flowing from one corner of Jesse's mouth. Convinced that Jesse James was dead, Becher sprang back up into his saddle and rode away, not only from the scene of ambush but from William Clarke Quantrill — for ever.

Unconscious on the ground, hidden by the darkness, Jesse James didn't know that Mel Becher had come back, through a hail of lead, to help him. Had he known this, maybe it would have made some difference when the two of them met again more than a decade later, maybe it wouldn't. Coughing blood, in agony because a musket ball had lodged in his lung, Jesse crawled slowly through the darkness.

Later, much later, exhausted by the painful crawl, soaked with perspiration as well as blood, Jesse reached the homestead of a kindly family by the name of Budd. They took him in, tended his wounds, nursed him back to health, then innocently released the dangerous Jesse James back into the world.

2

ON a scorching afternoon in the summer of 1876, five men rode in single file along the railway track that ran between St Louis and Little Rock, Arkansas. The horses moved slowly, the men were unspeaking. In the lead, head drooping but with an alertness that wouldn't fool the initiate in violence, was Mel Becher, aged thirty-five now, hardened and honed through the years, and with a reputation that had the less courageous slink away, and the would-be hero think twice before going for his gun, and his second thought was always the last. Behind him, also fast with a gun, was Johnny Cairew, his one-eighth Indian blood evident in high cheekbones and glossy blue/black hair. Young and ambitious, Cairew was prevented from challenging Becher for

15

leadership by a knowledge of his own limited capabilities compared to those of the older man, and a respect for Becher that had moved into the realms of hero-worship. The third man was a Mexican, dark-skinned and too ready to laugh in the most dangerous of situations, known only as Pedro.

Making up the rear were the two Stringer brothers, Ike and Cabel, both young, both slow thinkers, but both men who could handle themselves in a fight. The five had been together for more than two years, four of them had come to know each other well; yet none of them really knew their leader, the remote Mel Becher.

Reining his horse to a lethargic halt, Becher partly raised a listless hand to stop the men behind him. This was his way, a detached, uninterested style even in the tightest of situations, which they just couldn't get used to. Often it would seem that he just didn't care, had given up and they would all be caught, but he got them out of danger every time.

Up ahead, made indistinct by a shimmering of heat, was the station of Gads Hill. This was their destination. Becher just wanted them to look, to mentally digest the sight in some way, and then he was moving them on once more, at the same slow pace. As they drew closer an elderly negro outside of the station building rolled his eyes whitely at them before going back, with total concentration, to the polishing of a brass lamp. They dismounted, hitching their horses to a rail at the side of the building as the stationmaster, middle aged and badly frightened by their arrival, came out to stand looking at them.

"I'll have that," muttered Cabel Stringer, with a discreet nod at a gold watch-chain that was stretched across the ample middle of the stationmaster.

This had Pedro laugh shrilly, a sound that increased the fear on the stationmaster's face. He was clearing his throat, trying to find both the nerve and the voice to enquire as to their business, when Cairew effortlessly slid his .45 from its holster, just as easily and deftly pointing the barrel at the railwayman's thick middle.

"Keep the mouth closed, and get inside, mister," Cairew ordered.

With the stationmaster leading, Cairew's gun in his back, they all filed round the corner to the door of the building, the negro rolling his eyes as they passed, promising, "I ain't going to give you no trouble."

"That's for sure!" Ike Stringer grinned at the terrified black man, which caused Pedro to peal off another shrill laugh.

They locked the mildly protesting stationmaster in a large cupboard, dragging a heavy table across the floor to jam the doors as an extra precaution, then tied the negro, who was still making promises of co-operation, to a post in the corner of the room. Going outside, Pedro set the semaphore signal for the southbound train to stop.

Then they waited for the train from

St Louis. Cairew, the man with the sharpest hearing, stood in the doorway listening, his back against the jamb, while Becher leaned nonchalantly on the counter inside, not joining in the subdued conversation of the other three gang members who squatted on the floor.

An alerting hiss came from Cairew, which had Becher straighten up to check his rifle, draw his .45 from its holster, spin the chamber for a visual check before dropping it back into place. Neither Pedro or either of the Stringers had moved. They would believe nothing but their own senses, and Becher, who wanted to be prepared, gestured for the trio to stand up and join him beside Cairew, just inside the door.

The train could be heard now, puffing steadily at a regular speed, then, as if the engine itself was surprised, slowing. It arrived, wheels squealing on the tracks, steam escaping with an angry sound, as the engineer, a small, red-faced man, climbed down to stamp irately towards the station.

Becher and Cairew stepped out to confront the man, whose sharp query of "Where's . . ." was cut off by them covering him with their rifles. Becher told him tersely, but in a quiet voice, "Just take it easy, old man, and nobody will get hurt. You'll soon be on your way."

This was true. Becher, as always, had planned this well so that his non-shooting policy could be maintained. Once the gang had carried out its work the train would be allowed to leave. With the nearest telegraph apparatus being at Piedmont, Missouri, Becher and his men would be well gone before news of the holdup had been transmitted to Little Rock.

Leaving Ike Stringer covering the engineer, and a black conductor who had come running along the train to discover the reason for halting it, Becher directed the other Stringer brother and Pedro to tackle the safe in the express car, while he and Cairew moved into the coaches to relieve the passengers of their valuables.

They had an easy run, with Becher having only to use his .45 as a threat, and Johnny Cairew did the collecting. Trembling in fear, the passengers dug deeply, too frightened to hold anything back, and even a cavalry sergeant, a tough-looking *hombre* from whom Becher anticipated some degree of opposition, quietly passed over what must have been three months' wages. It was when they reached the last seats in the third coach that trouble came, from a most unexpected source.

A young girl, black haired, beautiful, and elegantly dressed, ignored Becher's gun and looked angrily straight into his eyes. Beside her sat a man of about her own age. He was also expensively dressed, and, like his companion, was obviously from back East, but he had nothing of her self-assurance, there being a slight tremor to his body as Cairew, an intimidating sight, signalled for him to pass over all valuables.

"Wait," said the girl, putting a gloved, restraining hand on the young man's arm as he was about to reach into his pockets. Then she addressed Becher. "You'll get nothing further from me. You have already taken the life of my father!"

A bewildered Becher frowned, shaking his head a little as he told her, "You've got me there, miss. I don't reckon I ever met your father."

"That's the sort of answer I'd expect from you," the girl snorted her derision. "Perhaps I should introduce myself. I am Rita Martin. My father was Silas Martin, executive of the Deposit Bank of Columbia in Adair County, which is where you shot him dead, Jesse James."

Beside him, Cairew gave a little snigger of amusement, but the mistaken identity, and hearing that name spoken after all the years that had passed, took Mel Becher aback. He had learned, of course, that Jesse hadn't been dead that night, but had survived to team up with Frank James and the Younger brothers to form a robber band that was feared throughout the land, but the world of the man he had ridden with under Quantrill had remained remote to Becher, until that moment.

There was a stirring behind him as the already robbed passengers twisted in their seats to look at Becher with renewed interest, and he heard the name 'Jesse James' being bandied about in whispers. It was a situation that could easily get out of hand, but he could rely on Johnny Cairew, who hefted the loot into one hand and drew his six-shooter with the other.

"Sit still and stay quiet," Cairew shouted the order, and was immediately obeyed.

Rita Martin was still staring at Becher, hatred now mingling with the anger in her eyes, and he, who had never felt the need to explain himself to anyone at any time, heard himself gruffly telling her, "I am not Jesse James."

She didn't believe him. Her expression and the way she held her head told him that, and he wanted to turn away because he could feel how much she despised him, and it hurt. Having lost interest in this little interchange, Cairew was again gesturing for the young man to give up his money and valuables. From outside, further down the train, came a call from Pedro. The safe had been emptied. There was nothing to hold them here now.

"Leave these two," he told Cairew, who didn't like the order, but obeyed it.

The two of them had turned when he heard the girl screech, "Coward!"

She had landed on Becher's back, clinging to his shoulders like a mountain lion, her fingers digging in, trying to rip his jacket, wanting to tear at him. Drawing his .45 again, Cairew reversed it in his mind, ready to swing it, using butt as a club to smash Rita Martin off the back of his leader.

"Johnny," snapped Becher, forbidding his deputy from taking his planned action. So rattled was Becher by the situation that he, for the first time ever, broke the golden rule of never uttering the name of an accomplice during a robbery.

One of the girl's hands was clawing into his hair now, while the other dug ridges into the skin of his neck. Becher felt his blood flow, but didn't experience pain. He had to do something to free himself. The sergeant further down the coach was on his feet now, facing them, a gun he had somehow concealed when he was searched, trained upon Becher, who was aware that the only reason the sergeant hadn't gunned him down was the fear of hitting the girl.

Becher was preparing to swing his right elbow into the girl's ribs. He was reluctant to do so, but he had no choice. If someone else joined the sergeant, then the lives of his four gang members and himself could well be at risk.

But he was saved from a move that would have severely injured Rita Martin, by her companion coming forward to show surprising strength for such a slightly-built guy by pulling the girl off Becher. This was all that the sergeant had been waiting for. Becher could see the soldier's finger tightening on the trigger, and he heard Cairew's urgent shout at his side, "Down!"

Wasting not a fraction of a second, Becher dived behind the seat to his right, hearing the crack of a shot and the screams of women, and feeling the sharp breath of the bullet that passed close to the left side of his head. There had been another shot, close to simultaneous, and Becher raised his head, the smell of cordite in his nostrils, hysterical screaming in his ears, to see the sergeant clutching at his midriff as he doubled over slowly, then sank to the floor of the coach.

Johnny Cairew had done his job,

and had done it well, but Becher was unhappy. He liked jobs to go cleanly, with no killing. While recognizing that the sergeant would have got him had not Cairew acted, Becher considered the shooting of the sergeant to be a bad omen.

When he hurried from the coach with Cairew, Becher felt the baleful glare of the girl on his back. She hadn't struggled when her companion had pulled her from Becher, and now she was standing beside the young man, not in need of any kind of restraint.

"What was the shooting?" Pedro wanted to know as they joined him and the others.

"Later," snapped Becher, waving to the engineer and the conductor to get back on board. "Get moving."

As the engine roared out steam, and the wheels spun sparking on the tracks before getting a grip, Cabel Stringer came up to Becher, excitement in his voice as he announced the total stolen from the safe. "Three thousand five hundred dollars."

It was a good haul, and Cairew and himself had done pretty well in the coaches, he knew that. Yet, try though he did, Becher couldn't let the good news out here come anywhere near balancing out the bad experience in the coach.

He was even more silent than usual as the train rolled slowly by, rumbling and hissing, carrying the fiery Rita Martin to God knew where, but still leaving much of her inside of the head of Mel Becher. There were three coaches yet to pass as Ike Stringer brought their horses round to them, and Becher willed the mental picture he had of the girl to be gone by the time the last coach had gone by.

The train had passed, the silence it left behind novel enough to be uncanny, and Cairew's shouted warning seemed to reach Becher from out of an echo chamber of some kind. He could tell the way that the part-Indian said his name that there was danger, and he came alert instantly.

"Mel," Johnny Cairew had called, and Becher swung round as he saw the man's black eyes focused on something behind him.

There, on the other side of the track, stood Rita Martin and her young companion. They were no more than seven feet from Becher, and he was first starkly aware of the frantic expression on the face of the slim young man, but he knew that the man wasn't the subject of Cairew's shout of caution. Becher shortened his gaze to take in the girl, who was standing a little in front of her companion.

The lovely face of Rita Martin was ashen, her eyes burning hotly at Becher. Her arms were stretched out in front of her, face high, and a derringer pistol was clasped steadily in both of her hands, the black hole of the muzzle, tiny but deadly, pointing at the heart of Mel Becher.

3

IF Zachary Waugh had been allowed
to pick a son-in-law, which he
hadn't, it certainly wouldn't have
been the fair-haired, bragging, lying
Chet Wheeler. But he'd been the
choice of sweet little Ruby, his only
child and a good gal to her daddy all
her life, so Zachary guessed that he'd
just have to make the best of it. At least
she hadn't left home, but had brought
her husband, a local boy, out here to
the Waugh homestead to live. Not that
there was enough work for two men,
which meant that Chet had to work for
the Circle M, a nearby ranch owned by
Jacob McNee. This was a good thing,
as it kept Wheeler away all day every
day, so Zachary didn't have to put up
with the youngster's stupid talk.

He knew that Ruby was hurt by her
father's attitude to her husband, and

he regretted that, because he loved his redheaded daughter dearly, but he still couldn't take to the boastful Chet. He had a suspicion, too, that Ruby guessed that a lot of his bias against her husband stemmed from his disappointment that she hadn't married the man he would have welcomed into the family. From the very first time Mel Becher had holed up here between jobs, him living in the house with them, his men sleeping in the barn, the outlaw and Ruby had hit it off right well. Zachary had, on a cosy night before Wheeler had come on the scene, when he and his daughter had sat talking by the fire, tentatively broached the subject of her becoming something more than a friend to Becher. He had taken care not to mention marriage, but she had known what he meant, and had brought it into the conversation herself.

"Tell me, Daddy," she had challenged him in that serious way she had, which made her pretty face look stronger than you'd expect in a girl her age, "what would you say if I came home and told you that I wanted to marry Cole, Jim, or Bob Younger?"

"We ain't discussing the Youngers boys: we're talking about Mel Becher," he had protested.

"No Daddy. We're talking about outlaws."

As usual, she had made her point in a way that was difficult to argue against, but he had tried with, "Mel's different, child. He's looking to settle down, and me and him could really make something of this place together."

"He'd settle down, all right," she smiled in a way that betrayed how fond she was of Becher, "until he got the urge to do another robbery."

It had ended there, and was as far as he'd ever got to playing matchmaker between the outlaw and his daughter. It wasn't really right to call Mel an outlaw, for he wasn't like the Jameses and the Youngers who were notorious. Frank James, in particular, so Zachary had heard, was a dangerous man when he had taken drink. In a lawless land like this you couldn't blame men who took what they wanted off those who had more than they did. Zachary Waugh rejoiced every time he heard of a bank being robbed, because never had a bank done him any favours. He had never had anything to do with railways, but he reckoned they'd be respectable criminals just like the banks were.

Anyway, Mel Becher didn't go in there blasting and shooting. Some of those men of his, especially the one with the Apache look, Johnny Cairew, were hard cases, but Becher kept them in line. In the opinion of Zachary Waugh there wasn't a man to equal Mel Becher.

Maybe it would have worked out the way he wanted if Nellie hadn't died giving birth to Ruby. A mother would probably have had more influence, but, there again, what mother would choose a gang leader as a husband for her daughter?

Resigning himself to his daughter's marriage, for the thousandth time, Zachary was reminded of his misery when he heard Chet's loud voice as Ruby and him came back from town in the sulky.

"It would set us up in a nice spread of our own," Chet, who'd never owned more than one pair of trousers, was saying as they came in through the door.

"What's that?" Zachary asked from where he sat mending a set of harness, curiosity defeating his better judgement.

Ruby, a real picture in her bright red dress, came over and kissed the top of her father's grey head. "Sheriff McDonald's got a poster up in town, offering five thousand dollars reward for the James gang, Daddy."

Striking a dramatic pose in the centre of the room, Chet told them, "I was as close to Frank James as I am to you two the other day. He passed me on the sidewalk." Making the motion of going for an imaginary gun in a pretend holster on his thigh, he added, "I should have just gunned him down."

Zachary was permitting himself a good laugh inside of his head, when Ruby spoilt his amusement by going over to place a hand on her husband's arm, the words she said causing her father to agonize on how such a clever girl could be taken in by a silly young braggart like Wheeler.

"Don't you ever take a chance with someone like Frank James, Chet," she pleaded. "You promise me?"

Giving it some thought, as if calling a man like Frank James was no problem to him, Chet at last gave a grudging nod of consent, which Ruby gratefully accepted.

What, Zachary caused personal distress by asking himself the question, would Mel Becher say when he next arrived and found that Ruby had married? Worse still, what would the tough Becher think of Chet Wheeler? Miserably, Zachary told himself that Mel would simply dismiss the stupid kid, ignore him altogether, which was something Zachary himself would love to be able to do.

This brought another thought to his mind — how would Wheeler react to Becher being here for the gang leader certainly would arrive one day? What was safest, Zachary wondered, warn the kid in advance, or leave it until Becher turned up? He decided on the first, and broached the subject when they were around the table that evening.

"Has Ruby mentioned to you Mel Becher stays with us from time to time, Chet?"

Chet Wheeler ate the way he did everything else, with too much mouth, and Zachary had to wait for a reply while his son-in-law noisily chewed on an overload of food. "Mel Becher? He ain't much, is he! Not like Sam Bass, the Jameses, the Youngers, or even Clem Miller."

Having dismissed Zachary's friend, Chet went back to his animated eating, leaving the older man fuming. No one, not even Chet Wheeler, should be allowed to criticize a man like Becher, but Zachary fought to stay quiet, and won, at a price. To say anything would be to upset his daughter, and that was something he would never knowingly do.

He contented himself with a jibe. "How would you go about getting Frank James, boy, bush-whack him?"

"Chet's promised . . . " Ruby began, but her husband, too conceited to recognize that he was being ribbed, came back hotly at his father-in-law.

"I don't have to bushwhack no one. I'd do the same with Frank James as I would any other man — face him!"

"I'd sooner try catch a rattler by the tail," Zachary said, while he worried about the boy. The talk about facing one of the Jameses was, of course, just bravado, but he had more than a sneaking suspicion that his son-in-law would sell a man down the river, any man, perhaps Mel Becher, for the reward.

They finished the meal, sitting at the table still, resting, when Will McDonald came in, shouting his hellos. The sheriff was around the same age as Zachary, and they had been friends, although not close ones, for years.

"What brings you out this way, Will?"

"Just passing." The sheriff nodded at Chet, gave Ruby a warm smile, and pointed questioningly to a chair. "May I?"

You don't have to ask to sit in my house," Zachary told him cordially, and the sheriff sat, taking out a pipe and tobacco.

"I reckon you smelled food, Sheriff McDonald," Ruby's eyes twinkled. "I guess I can find enough to feed you."

Breaking off from packing the pipe, McDonald raised a big hand to stay the girl. "Right kind of you, Miss Ruby, but I ate at Ma Dingle's before I left town."

This had Zachary realize that the sheriff had ridden straight out, and he was suspicious. "Where ye heading, Will?"

Will McDonald was puffing so hard as he lit his pipe that he didn't seem to hear Waugh's question, and Zachary lacked the nerve to repeat it. With the bowl of the pipe glowing, and the aroma of tobacco smoke filling the room, the sheriff said in a conversational way, "They robbed a train up at Gads Hill today, Zach. Bad business. Killed a sergeant from the 7th Cavalry."

"Get away with much, Sheriff?" Chet asked.

"An awful lot of money, son," McDonald replied gravely.

"Sounds like the James boys," Zachary volunteered, but the sheriff gave a negative shake of his large head.

"Not this time, Zach. There ain't no doubt that it was Mel Becher. Stationmaster and several others recognized him."

Zachary Waugh went suddenly weak,

a feeling akin to the illness that had laid him low for a week or more a couple of winters ago. But this wasn't an illness now, but a deep feeling of dread. He wanted to correct the sheriff, tell him that though Mel Becher was a robber he wasn't a killer. But McDonald was nobody's fool, and he'd latch on to a remark like that.

"The thing is," Will McDonald continued, "that when the gang rode off they took two young people with them."

Hearing this made Zachary feel worse than ever. Neither murder nor kidnapping was Becher's style, and he was ready to question this, but Chet, whose mind always ran on a money track, saved him the bother.

"They'll be asking a huge ransom, I reckon!"

McDonald shook his head. "Not much point in it. These two aren't children. The young man," — he referred to a note in his pocket, — "Iain Fulton, was on his way out West to run a bank in Gallatin, Missouri. The young woman, as I understand it, is his fiancée."

"What is her name?" Ruby asked illogically and unnecessarily.

"I'm afraid I don't know that, miss." The sheriff gave a wry grin. "All I knows is that there's a mighty big hunt on for them."

This was bad news, Zachary knew. Though a pain in the side because of the robberies he carried out, society hadn't turned against Mel Becher the way they had the Jesse James' gang, but it looked as if that had all changed now, and he couldn't understand why Mel had shot the sergeant and taken the two young people captive.

"Is that why you're out here, Sheriff?" Chet Wheeler enquired, asking the question that was uppermost in Zachary's mind.

"No, son," McDonald scoffed. "Mel Becher ain't never hung around these parts, and I don't reckon he's likely to turn up here now."

This sounded genuine enough, but there was a look on McDonald's face, and a light in the eyes he turned on to Zachary Waugh, that was most disturbing.

4

THERE was not the slightest shake in the girl's hands holding the pistol, and her aim at Becher was accurate. Never having met such a situation, with a female at the other end of a gun, the business end, he was flummoxed, just standing still and waiting for the inevitable. The fury in the eyes of Rita Martin told him that she was going to shoot, and he calmly resigned himself to that.

"OK, Mel, I've got her covered."

The voice of Ike Stringer came to him from behind. Moving his head slightly, Becher could see Ike beside the horses, rifle to his shoulder, aimed at the girl.

"Rita, please," the young man beside her begged.

"Stay quiet, Iain," she told him firmly, then, with the same tone of conviction, she said to Becher, "Your man will get me, I don't doubt that, but not before I kill you, Jesse James!"

"What's she talking about?" an astounded Ike asked, though he didn't lower his rifle.

"She's loco," Cairew put in. "She reckons Mel is Jesse."

Pedro laughed his shrill laugh which, if anything, added to the tension rather than relieved it. Becher took some comfort from the fact that the girl had not yet pulled the trigger, but she did look capable of doing so at any moment.

"Listen, missy," Johnny Cairew addressed the girl without making a move, not wanting her to misconstrue any action of his, which might well result in the death of Mel Becher, "this here ain't no Jesse James, not by a long chalk he ain't."

"Listen, whoever you are. I don't frighten easily, neither do I fool easily," the girl hissed.

"Then you're making a right fool of

44

yourself right now, missy," Cairew half mocked Rita Martin.

An idea occurred to Becher, and he called softly to Ike Stringer, "Go get the stationmaster, Ike. Bring him out here."

As Stringer went inside the station building, a frown came to the brow of Rita Martin, but she still held the gun on Becher, while her male companion showed signs of greater agitation.

"I don't know what you're trying to do," she warned Becher, "but it won't make any difference. I won't give you any more of a chance than you gave my father."

Becher stayed quiet, while his men exchanged puzzled glances, and then Ike came out of the building, pushing the indignant stationmaster ahead of him, the negro running out beside them.

Jerking his head in the direction of the stationmaster, Becher told the girl, "Ask him who I am."

Without lowering her tiny pistol, the

girl thought this invitation over, and when she did take it up, she worded it her way.

"This man is Jesse James, isn't he?"

This made the negro railway worker, no longer as terrified as he had been, chortle, and the stationmaster shook a bewildered head. Adding to it all with his shrill laugh, Pedro completed a scene that had the girl totally bemused.

"This here man ain't Jesse James," the stationmaster gruffly informed the girl. He wasn't a happy man, having just been an indirect victim of a robbery that could well cost him his job.

As she slowly lowered her arms, the girl's face collapsed, and her companion stepped forward to take her into his arms. She buried her face against the young man's shoulder, watched by a motionless Becher who was experiencing an unprecedented spell of inertia that was perplexing his men and caused Cairew to prompt him, "We'd best get moving, Mel."

"You're right, Johnny," Becher agreed,

coming back to life and leading the way to the horses.

They were mounting up when the young man left the girl and walked to Becher's side. "Excuse me, I'm Iain Fulton. You already know the name of my fiancée. We regret the misunderstanding, and wondered if you could find it possible to help us. You see, we are on our way to Gallatin."

"You were, until you got off the train, *señor*," Pedro laughed wildly at his own wit.

"It is most important that we reach the town," said Fulton.

"Right now, mister," Johnny Cairew leaned over in his saddle to speak to the Easterner, "it's most important that we avoid the sheriff's posse that will be heading this way."

Ignoring this banter, the young man still had pleading eyes on Becher, who asked, "Can you ride?"

"I can manage it," Fulton let his failings as a horseman make him sound indecisive.

"And her?" Becher nodded to where the now forlorn figure of the girl stood.

"Miss Martin was a member of a stable back East."

Sensing the justified impatience of his men, Becher looked ahead at the horizon, while Fulton pressed him, "Can you take us at least part of the way?"

Cairew told Fulton, "Having been riding somewhere back East won't help much out here, mister."

With an abashed expression on her perfect features, Rita Martin walked over to stand beside her fiancé, not looking at Becher, who was deep in thought, and then Becher said, "You can ride with us a spell."

"Mel," Cairew made a protest out of the way he said the word.

"We've got the horses." Becher gestured with his head to the spare mounts they always brought with them in case of relentless pursuit. "Ike, you and your brother let them have your saddles."

Though the men did as they were ordered, there was much muttered objection. Riding bare-back would be no hardship for the Stringer brothers, who were both exceptional horsemen, but they were reluctant to be slowed down by a couple of greenhorns, one of them a woman, at that. It was Pedro who voiced a complaint.

"It is bad luck to have a *señorita* along."

"Specially if she tries to blow your head off again, Mel," Cairew commented laconically. He saw having the Easterners ride with them as a diversion, and he wasn't worried, because he'd known Mel Becher long enough to trust his judgement in anything and everything. He guessed that Becher was feeling sorry for the girl, and Cairew suspected that the petite and beautiful girl had reached some soft centre in hard-man Becher.

That wasn't easy to do. Being a man, the gang leader had visited professional girls at times, but, though there had been several women after him, Becher had never before shown signs of being vulnerable to a female presence. Johnny Cairew looked forward with interest to what would unfold as they rode.

Out of necessity, they rode fast, and it was equally as hard on Iain Fulton as it was on his fiancée. But she kept moving without protest, riding abreast with Fulton behind Becher and Cairew, ahead of Pedro and the Stringers. By covering a lot of ground in a short time, they could light a fire in the arroyo where they camped for the night, heating coffee and beans, secure in the knowledge that no posse could be within miles of them.

Sitting close together on the opposite side of the fire the desperadoes, Rita Martin and Iain Fulton smiled their thanks briefly when Pedro brought them coffee and food. Both of them had begun to look more and more frightened as the darkness grew thicker. Now they were disorientated by night on the vastness of the prairie, and alarmed by every sound made by a creature of darkness.

When the meal was over, Pedro reached into a shirt pocket for a harmonica. When he played, skilfully, the plaintive tune of mourning for a time gone by, 'Empty Saddles in the Old Corral', drifted sadly on the still air, and a poignant atmosphere was increased as Cabel Stringer, who had a more than passable voice, sang the lyrics.

Ending the song, Pedro struck up the lively 'Turkey in the Straw', playing just a few bars before giving up, letting loose a laugh, and saying, "I reckon as how nobody wants to dance."

"Here's one tired *hombre* who wants to sleep." Johnny Cairew told the Mexican, sliding down so that his head rested on his saddle, stetson over his face.

Getting to his feet, Becher selected some blankets from his saddle-roll and walked round the fire to pass one each to the young couple, not speaking as

51

they murmured their grateful thanks. He was back where he intended to sleep, laying his rifle and his unholstered .45 together where they would be in easy reach, when the girl walked up to speak softly.

"I owe you a big apology," she said, embarrassed by her own earlier behaviour, unnerved by his presence.

Still busy with his preparations for the night, Becher delayed his reply, and when it came it was just two words. "No need."

"But there is," Rita Martin argued self-consciously. "I tried to kill you, and I accused you of being Jesse James."

Unfolding a blanket and laying it out on the ground, Becher spoke to her in his low-voiced way. "You thought about killing me, because you thought I'd murdered your father — there's a lot of difference between those two things, ma'am. As for the other, I guess that being in the same business as Jesse James means your mistake wasn't much of an insult."

There was a dismissal of her in the way he ended the last sentence, but there was something on her mind that made her reluctant to go. Finding courage from deep inside of herself, she risked rebuff by saying more. "I heard your men talking as we rode today. The shooting of that soldier is something that you wouldn't have wanted to happen, wasn't it?"

Becher shrugged, realized that she couldn't see the gesture in the dark, so said, "It's done, and that's it."

"It was my fault," the girl sounded almost tearful. "It is my fault that he died."

"Dead is dead," Becher told her, being deliberately callous by adding, "Reckon as how it doesn't make any difference to that sergeant why he's dead, because as I said, dead is dead."

She was moving away, acutely aware that he wanted her to go, but she paused, turned, and spoke curiously, "You're a mystery man. Your command of grammar belies your way of life."

"Just shows you what a bad thing education can be," he replied enigmatically, then lay down as a signal that there would be no further conversation.

Going back to where her blanket was placed, still folded, on the ground, she found her fiancé rolled and snug in his, and called softly to him, "Are you awake, Iain?"

"Yes."

"I'm frightened," she confessed. "I don't know what I've got us into."

"Whatever it is, we're in it together," he told her gallantly, but she could detect a tremor of uneasiness in his voice.

She was wrapping herself in the blanket when he spoke, his tone betraying his unhappiness. "Why did you go over to speak to that man?"

"To apologize."

"Did he accept your apology?"

Lying down now, finding herself ready for sleep despite the spartan conditions, she had to give a lot of thought to the question Iain had asked. Never had she met a man like the gang leader. Though she could sense that he would do them no harm, her inexperience of his tough type made her uncertain. She was, in fact, uncertain about everything concerning the man she had learned was Mel Becher.

"I don't know," she replied honestly, after an interval so protracted that her fiancé had given up on getting an answer.

"We should have waited at that place — what was it called?"

"Gads Hill," she told him.

"We should have waited there for the next train," he complained.

Rita Martin raised herself up on one elbow to tell him, "There would have been too long a delay. Judge Lewis leaves Gallatin at noon the day after tomorrow, you know that. If you are not there to take up the appointment before that, then it could cost you your job at the bank. I don't think we'd have got to the town in time that way."

"I think we'll be lucky to make it to Gallatin at all this way," he told her miserably, and that was the last they spoke to each other that night.

They were rudely awoken at dawn the next morning. They saw the gang moving about urgently in a low mist that chilled both the ground and their bones. There would be no coffee, nothing to eat. They had to mount up, they learned, as Johnny Cairew had gone out scouting in the early hours, and had just ridden back to report that a massive sheriff's posse was approaching fast.

"That dang-blasted sergeant," Pedro cursed as he went about his chores, making Rita Martin feel guilty because she knew that he blamed the size and the closeness of the posse on the soldier being shot.

As they mounted up, the members of the gang saying little to each other, and nothing at all to Rita Martin and Iain Fulton, she kept looking in the direction of Mel Becher, expecting him

56

to acknowledge her with at least a nod of his head, but she might as well not have been there for all the notice he took.

They rode hard throughout the forenoon, the strain on the girl so intense that she feared that she couldn't go on, while Iain Fulton, not made for the hard life or horse-riding, looked close to collapse as he clung to the mane of his horse in order to remain in the saddle. It was Pedro who brought the matter to a head. Passing the two Easterners, he joined Becher and Cairew, riding along beside them.

"It's no good, Mel," the Mexican called. "They're slowing us down."

Cairew nodded in agreement. "We've got to move on, Mel. Leave the kids here. They ain't got nothing to fear from the posse, and we know they'll be taken care of."

They rode on for a while, with Becher deep in thought. What his two companions said made absolute sense, and he couldn't understand, nor come to terms with, the strange feeling deep inside of himself that made it so difficult to part from Rita Martin. But it had to be, and the others reined in as he pulled up his horse, wheeled the animal and walked it back to explain the situation to the young couple.

"The sheriff's men will take care of you both," he assured them, not looking at the girl, adding for his own benefit, "There was no way we could have known that the chase would start so soon and move so fast."

Though the young man looked relieved, the girl was obviously saddened by the change of plan. With an eye to the practical side of things, Ike Stringer, as they were about to move off, leaving the couple behind, reminded Becher, "What about our horses, Mel?"

"Let them keep them," Becher instructed, but he couldn't deprive his men of their saddles, and he told the Stringers to take them. Standing side by side in the heat, the two

Easterners, aware that they had no say in what was to happen to them, looked unhappy. Though dishevelled and streaked with dust, Rita Martin maintained her beauty, and when the Stringers had buckled their saddles on to their horses, she looked directly at Becher, a question in her eyes.

Hesitating, he held her gaze, while Cairew's eyes darted anxiously from Becher to a rocky escarpment that would be on their left as they rode away. Cairew was in no doubt that a couple of good men from the posse, on fast horses, could have flanked them by now, and be able to pick them off as they headed for the pass up ahead. He called to his leader urgently, "Mel!"

Becher nodded, seemingly to himself, as if agreeing with something said by an inner voice. Without speaking, but with his gaze holding that of the girl up to the last moment, he wheeled his horse, spurring the animal to follow Cairew. The Stringers and Pedro were already making dust a fair distance ahead.

The crack of a rifle and the result of the shot were so close that Becher couldn't separate them in his mind. He felt the stride of his horse check, then regain its former pace, before the animal dropped head-first, somersaulting, snorting a last, blood-gurgling breath as it hit the ground, but throwing Becher, who had instinctively freed his feet from the stirrups, clear. Though winded by the fall, he recovered himself, looking around him in search of cover as a slug whined past him — very close. There was a cluster of small rocks beside him, the protection they offered too scant to be of any use, but he wriggled towards them. A bullet hit a rock beside him sending splinters of jagged stone to slash at his face. Whoever was on the other end of the rifle was good: so good that the next shot would mean the end for Becher, he knew that. Despite their loyalty, none of the others would come back, for it would be suicidal to do so. Then he heard the pound of hooves approaching fast, and he cursed Cairew for a fool, giving his own life on a hopeless mission.

Waiting for the next shot, wondering if it would just bring blackness or awareness and pain, Becher eased his head to one side where he clung to the ground, desperate eyes seeking the rider.

He saw her then! Rita Martin, a wild look to her as her black hair blew behind her, riding a saddleless horse as easily as any Indian, was bearing down on him. Wanting to shout to her, he found his mouth and throat too dry for words to be uttered. But he had to warn her, because she was in great danger. Thoughtless of the danger to himself, he got first to his knees and then to a crouching stand as the girl rode in close to him, the horse's hooves skidding through the dust as she reined it to an abrupt halt.

Swinging down off the horse's back, she hissed at Becher, "Ride!"

He couldn't do it. No way could

he mount up and leave her there, probably to take the next bullet fired. The rifleman was obviously waiting to see how this odd situation developed.

"Ride!" Rita said again, spitting the word at him through her white teeth, urging him to do as she said.

Then he saw the logic of it. Not to take the horse would be to make it so she had risked her life for nothing. It wasn't wrong to do as she said — but it would be wrong not to. He ran, leapt to straddle the horse, and kicked his heels into its ribs. The animal was off at a gallop. Bullets whistled past Becher, but the speed he rode at made him a difficult target.

Soon he was out of range, at least for the time being, and he allowed himself to turn his head and look back. Distance made the girl little more than a dot, but he could see that she was upright and unharmed, walking back to another dot where Iain Fulton stood.

5

JUDGE LEWIS, one of the executives of the bank in Gallatin, was a fussy little man who found it impossible not to wear a constant smile while in the presence of a woman. That smile was there now as he walked from the back office of the bank with Iain Fulton and Rita Martin, having greeted them both enthusiastically, and welcoming Iain as manager.

"I was honoured to number your late father as one of my dearest friends, Miss Martin," he said managing to twist his smile momentarily into a sorrowing expression as they entered the public section of the bank, where two tellers, both males, were busy with queues of customers. "It was such a tragedy, so callous a wasting of life. If it is any consolation to you, we have contributed to the reward offered for the James gang."

The girl murmured her false appreciation of this, as a contribution towards a reward didn't in any way measure up to the loss of a father, the shattering of a family, for her mother was to have come out West with her and Iain, joining her father. Now a bullet from an uncaring bank raider had ended all that.

"Have you found suitable accommodation in town, Miss Martin?" Judge Lewis asked solicitously.

"I have rooms with Mrs Costain," she told him, looking around the busy bank, trying to imagine Iain being in full charge within a few days.

"Ah," exclaimed the judge in satisfaction. "You couldn't have found a better house in Gallatin, Miss Martin. Now, Iain, let me introduce you to your staff."

Not wanting to push in on Iain's business, Rita walked to a window, looking out on a street where people went about their business slightly bent against a strongish wind. Sagebrush whipped up through the thoroughfare occasionally, often entangling itself in the legs of walkers, who kicked it away, other times tumbling against the legs of horses tied to hitching rails, making the animals skittish.

Although Iain was with her, she felt disorientated and homesick in this western town. It would have been so very different had not her father been murdered. Admittedly, her parents would be living in Adair County, but they would be close and, most importantly, there wouldn't be this aching, sad part of her heart where her father should be.

Two customers, tough-looking men who she guessed would be ranchers, turned away from a table where they had been attending some business or other, almost colliding with her before noticing Rita standing there. They both respectfully touched their hats, and one said a quiet, "I beg your pardon, ma'am."

They went out of the door, and she

65

idly watched them make their bow-legged way down the street. In the far distance she could see a group of men wearing duster coats and standing beside their horses. She sensed, without knowing why, that the pair who had left the bank were walking to join that group. What she couldn't know was that the two men were the outlaws Clell Miller and Charlie Pitts.

Had not Iain called to her just then, wanting her to rejoin Judge Lewis and herself, Rita would have seen that her hunch was right, and the two men did walk up to the group at the end of the street, where they were passed the reins of their horses.

"Well?" asked Frank James, who was one of five men wearing duster coats.

"Easy as falling off a log." Clell Miller gave his stock answer in such situations, and the other James brother, Jesse, turned his bright, hard eyes to Pitts for a more reliable opinion.

The other three men, Cole, Jim and Bob Younger, were waiting for

Pitts' report, too. They lived dangerous lives, and had long ago learned that, regardless how many successful robberies they pulled off, the next one might be the end of any or all of them.

"Bank's easy enough," Pitts nodded, choosing his words with care because he was a miser with them. "Sheriff could be trouble."

"His name?" Jesse James asked sharply.

"McDonald."

Cole Younger raised a hand that held the reins of his horse. "I knows him, Jesse."

"A problem?"

It was Frank James who enquired. Besides being older, he was nothing like his brother in looks, which added to the guardedly whispered speculation that Jesse was a love child. Whether or not he was illegitimate, the question would never be asked in the presence of Jesse, or Frank for that matter. There wasn't much to choose between them. Jesse was normally cold and dangerous, whereas Frank became trigger-happy when he'd had a drink or two. Most people were wary of both of them, adhering to the old maxim that you never messed with the Jameses.

"I ain't never heard tell of Will McDonald facing anyone, but he ain't the sort of feller you'd want on your tail," Cole Younger drawled.

"He won't be on our tails," said Jesse confidently, before asking Miller, who had a sharp mind for finances, "When do we hit the bank, Clell?"

"There ain't no rush, Jesse, that's for sure." Miller looked thoughtful. "Depends what you're looking for; a couple of thousand dollars tomorrow, or ten to twelve thousand at the end of next week."

"I reckon . . . " Bob Younger started to give his opinion, but changed it, unconvincingly, into a clearing of his throat when Jesse swung his head angrily towards him.

"Reckon as how we'll wait," Jesse said, and that was it.

They mounted up, then rode slowly up the street together, not looking in the direction of the bank as they passed, but, out of the corner of his eye, Jesse saw the beautiful face of a woman looking out of the window. For a moment Jesse James, always alert and clear-headed, was confused, badly confused, for it seemed that it was the face of Zerelda, the cousin he loved and had married. This had him twist his head for a direct look, and he was satisfied. It wasn't his wife, but his eyes met those of this strange woman, and an inexplicable chill ran up his spine.

Then the bank was behind him, the eerie feeling all but gone, and he heard his brother speak as he nodded towards a saloon, which was as dead as buzzard-bait at that time of day.

"I guess it's going to be an awful long week, Jesse!"

His handsome face wearing a hint of a smile, Jesse James replied, "I reckon as how we could make ourselves look like ordinary cowpokes, and ride into town for some relaxation, brother Frank."

They rode on at a leisurely pace while, still at the window of the bank, Rita Martin watched them go. Before she had looked out at that man with the hard eyes she had been unsettled and, she had to admit, unhappy, but now she felt frightened. It showed on her face, too, because Iain was worried when he walked up to where she stood.

"What's the matter, Rita?" he asked anxiously. "You've gone very pale."

"It's nothing," she told her fiancé, a little flustered, then went to point a finger out of the window at the men who looked so disturbing in their long duster coats, but they were out of sight, and she was feeling foolish as Judge Lewis approached them, smiling his everlasting smile.

"Well, that's about it, Iain," the judge said. "I'm leaving town this afternoon, but I'm sure that you'll be able to manage. Both Peters and

Gibson are good men, and they'll help you with any difficulties you may encounter because of your newness here."

"When will you be back, sir?" Iain enquired, a little perplexed at having so much responsibility thrust on him so suddenly.

"Within a month," Judge Lewis assured him, then gave a cheeky little wink to support his smile as he added, "Unless, of course, some special occasion brings me back earlier!"

"I don't quite understand, sir?" said Iain.

Slapping him lightly and friendly on the shoulder, the judge looked at Rita as he said, "I was thinking that Miss Miller and yourself might be setting the date now that you've settled here in town. Now that is a wedding that I wouldn't like to miss!"

Blushing, Rita looked away as Iain stammered, "It won't be just yet, sir."

"Take my advice, don't leave it too long, son. Life is short, so make the most of it." The judge's cheeks juggled a little dance of amusement inside of the red/blue skin of his face. "There's a nice little house goes with this appointment, as you know."

Later, when the judge had gone and Iain joined her at Mrs Costain's she considered telling him that she didn't like Judge Lewis, but not only would that hurt her fiancé, who was so pleased with becoming manager of the bank, it would have meant that, in her truthful, direct way, she would have to continue that neither did she like it here in Gallatin and, worse still, add that she was rapidly fading away from the idea of marrying him.

For the past few hours she had been trying, unsuccessfully, to convince herself that this was an aberration brought about by their experiences on the journey here. She recognized that Iain had been shaken by the way she had helped the outlaw leader escape by taking the horse to him, but she appreciated her fiancé's silence on the matter. Had the man escaped? That was a question that persisted in her mind, and she was honest enough with herself to accept that the issue of whether Mel Becher had got safely away from the posse had, for her, taken priority over Iain's appointment at the bank.

There were so many things that she should tell him right then, to be fair to him, but Iain was so elated with taking the position of the manager of a bank, that all she could do was blurt out something that was totally unrelated.

"I saw a man today."

It was a simple, uninformative statement and, not surprisingly, Iain's face was puzzled across the table from her.

"It was when we were in the bank, and you were busy with Judge Lewis," she went on, knowing that she was talking too fast, but unable to slow her speech. "I was looking out of the window as he and some others went by on horseback."

"And?" Iain asked, pouring them both more tea, his white, well-cared for hands well suited to his impeccable dress.

"I'm sure it was the man who shot my father."

Now that she'd said it, it sounded just as silly as she had known it would, and her fiancé wore an exasperated expression as he studied her. "How on earth could you know that, Rita?"

"It's a feeling I have, deep down," she replied, aware that he could put her down by reminding her of how she had been equally as sure that Mel Becher was the murderer. He didn't: that wouldn't have been like Iain.

"It's been a traumatic time, Rita, and you are understandably overwrought." He gave her an encouraging little smile, reaching across the table to hold one of her hands. You'll settle down and feel much better in a day or two."

Closing her eyes in an attempt at calming herself, trying to get everything into perspective, Rita had a mental picture of the gang of men in long coats riding slowly up through the street. She saw the one she had taken to be the leader: young and incredibly handsome, who had looked so deeply into her eyes. The feeling that he was connected with the death of her father suddenly ebbed away, to be replaced by a terrible premonition. That man was a danger to Iain, a terrible menace that made her want to cry out in protest. She couldn't stand the death of another person close to her.

Should she warn him, she wondered? No, he wouldn't take her seriously, and who could blame him after her recent behaviour? She felt terribly guilty over her earlier thoughts about not wanting to marry Iain.

Wanting to beg him to take her back East, that very day, to leave here this instant, she had to content herself with an unasked for apology. "I'm sorry, Iain."

"You have nothing to be sorry for," he told her.

Somewhere in the distance, but still within the confines of this terrible town, there was the sound of a gunshot. Nerves strained to breaking point, Rita Martin gave an involuntary little scream.

6

THEY reached Zachary Waugh's place at dusk, Becher, the Stringers, and Pedro, sitting motionless on their horses in among a clump of trees several hundred yards from the house while Johnny Cairew went on in to reconnoitre. Always a cautious man, Mel Becher was additionally so when in Sheriff Will McDonald's district. Although McDonald wasn't a man he respected, he recognized that he was not only a capable lawman, but had some kind of obsession where he, Becher, was concerned. Zachary had noticed this, too, and Becher was glad of his friend's acquaintanceship with the sheriff, which enabled him to keep at least one step ahead.

Having given the posse the slip, Becher had been able to give some thought to the girl who had acted so unexpectedly to save his life. To see someone from back East, particularly a female, ride like that, straight into rifle fire, had been something he would never forget. But what Cairew had said at the camp-fire several nights later, had made him morose. The Indian in Johnny had come to the fore, as he'd looked into the fire while speaking to Becher.

"That woman owns you now, Mel."

The idea was abhorrent to Becher, but Cairew had said it with such a degree of feeling that it was difficult to shrug off, and Becher complained, more to reassure himself than to argue with his second-in command, "I don't figure it that way."

"There ain't no other way to figure it, Mel," Cairew was adamant. "She owns you lest you clear the debt."

"How would I do that?" Becher had asked, trying to make himself sound disinterested.

"Well now," Cairew considered the

problem. "A young buck in your position would decide to kill the person who owns him. I've seen it happen among the Cherokees, amigo. One brave has saved the life of another brave in battle, and it gets to the first buck so much that he frees himself by killing his saviour."

"That won't be a way out for me," Becher had said. Adding, "That is if I have to find a way out of anything, which I don't believe."

Cairew came back to them now, riding up to Becher. "There's a stranger here."

"What's his business?" a disappointed Becher asked quickly. This was bad news. He had been looking forward to long chats with Zachary, good food, and a comfortable bed.

"I guess you ain't going to like this, Mel, you ain't going to like it one little bit, amigo," Cairew carefully prepared him. "But it's some young *hombre* from hereabouts, and he's got himself hitched to Zachary's gal."

Although the poker-faced Becher never showed emotion, he was aware that Cairew was studying him closely now, searching for some sign of a reaction to the news he had brought from the Waugh homestead. It came as something of a shock for Becher to realize that it meant little or nothing to him. There was a time when he'd have been hurt to learn that Ruby, a girl he had been extremely fond of for years, had married, but now it left him untouched. It would have been different, he confessed to himself, had he not met the black-haired beauty that was Rita Martin.

"Is this man of Ruby's safe?" he asked, getting pleasure from the disappointment on the face of Cairew, who had been expecting a noticeable response.

"Zachary's mouth said that the boy can be trusted," Cairew said, frowning. "But there was something about old Zach's eyes that told me different."

Becher shared the latterly expressed

thought of his deputy when they were in the house and Zachary was pumping his hand in enthusiastic welcome. The boy introduced as Chet Wheeler had done his best to be friendly, but there was definitely something to him that Becher couldn't take to. As for Ruby, who was as pretty as ever, marriage hadn't done much for her. She was unusually nervous and awkward, although Becher reckoned that could be excused by her discomfort at having married someone else when there was a kind of unspoken agreement between her and Becher over the years, an agreement supported by, or possibly devised by, her father.

With Cairew at his side, Becher ate at the family table, while Ruby served the Stringers and Pedro their food out in the barn. When it was over, the good food making Becher and his sidekick sleepy, they enjoyed smoking the cigars Zachary passed around, hesitating, Becher noticed, when he held out the box to his new son-in-law. In this area Zachary could be relied upon to know what money lay where, and how easy or difficult it would be to get at so, as Ruby cleared the crocks away, Becher blew out cigar smoke and asked his host, "What have you for me, Zach?"

For a time it seemed that the older man hadn't heard him. Head back, his long grey hair reaching down over his collar, Zachary had his eyes shut as he inhaled cigar smoke, and Becher was about to repeat his question when his friend spoke without opening his eyes.

"Plenty of time for that sort of thing, Mel," Zachary said evasively.

It was then that Becher realized that Zachary didn't want to talk business in the company of Chet Wheeler, and Becher felt a little stupid, feeling sure that Cairew had grasped the situation some time before he had.

Later that evening, when Ruby came into the room and was about to sit, her father suggested, "Hadn't you better take a look at that milch cow before nightfall, girl!"

Ruby looked momentarily puzzled, and then, as her father explained to Becher and Cairew that they had an ailing animal, the girl got the subliminal message, and got to her feet, calling to her husband, "Come on, Chet, we'll go check her out."

"A good girl." Zachary nodded confirmation of his love for Ruby after she and Wheeler had left. "Wasted on that Wheeler crittur."

"Why did you let her marry him, Zach?" asked Cairew.

Zachary snorted. "Fathers don't have no say in that sort of thing these days, Johnny. You wait till you've got a girl of that age yourself."

"I reckon that would be a long wait," said Cairew laconically, while Becher, fearing that Chet Wheeler would soon be back, wanted to get down to business.

"How do you see things, Zach?"

"You sure are eager to do a job, Mel. What's up, didn't the ransom idea pay off?"

Becher frowned at his friend. "I ain't with you, Zach."

"Will McDonald dropped by here, told me you boys pulled off a good 'un at Gads Hill. Took a couple of hostages with you, by all accounts."

This had Cairew give a soft little laugh, as Becher went on to explain, telling Waugh the complete story, including how the girl had ridden up with a horse to save his life.

"Which means Mel ain't his own man no more, Zach." Cairew wagged his head gravely. "That little black-haired girl owns him now."

"Indian nonsense." Zach pulled a face of disgust.

"Don't you be too sure," said Cairew, still serious of face. "We don't take no notice of the kind of law that wears a badge, but there's laws in this world that have to be obeyed, and that there is one of them."

"I'm more interested in the law we know about," Becher told his second-in-command, then looked at Zachary.

"Why did McDonald come here?"

"Danged if I haven't been asking myself the same question since that time, Mel," Zachary replied. "I reckon as how he's got his suspicions about me and you."

"I don't like the sound of it." Becher looked worried, but Cairew moved things along.

"Like Mel asked, Zach," he said to the older man, "what's happening in your neck of the woods? I guess we'd better get down to business before your kin comes back in."

"Ruby's me kin, but don't you link me with that Wheeler feller," Zachary warned, revealing the depth of his feelings, or lack of them, for his son-in-law. "Now, Mel, you said that that girl of yourn, the one who tried to blow your skull off, was heading for Gallatin."

"You got it, Zach," Becher nodded without hesitation. He had given much thought to the girl and her destination.

"Then like as how you might run

85

into her again, Mel," — Zachary let a grin divide his strong, stern face — "because the bank at Gallatin would be well worth a visit late next week."

"How much?" asked Cairew with a misleading detachment.

"Some say ten, but it could be around fifteen thousand," Zachary answered, causing Cairew to give a long, low whistle of surprise.

Becher had straightened up in his chair, full of interest, but there were reservations in his tone as he commented, "Gallatin's McDonald country."

"True enough," Zachary concurred. "But Will, like myself, is a bit long in the tooth now, Mel, and past his best. Time it right and there won't be no shoot-out. If it comes to it, then Will McDonald ain't going to put on no big show. It ain't his style these days, boys. No, I'd bet my last dollar that old Will would keep low, then hunt you down afterwards."

"If we was to give him the chance," Cairew commented softly. "What deputies he got, Zach?"

"Just two: men with families, so they ain't gonna buck you none."

Flicking his cigar stub into the grate, Cairew raised an eyebrow at Becher. "What's the next move, Mel?"

"I reckon," Becher replied lazily, "that we'll have Ike Stringer go into Gallatin and take a look-see."

That's what happened the next morning. Ike rode out, leaving his brother and Pedro busy shoeing the horses, while Cairew, jogging easily on foot, went off into the hills to the west of the Waugh place. Not for the first time since Becher had known him, Johnny Cairew was in some way reverting to the Indian blood in him. He'll be back, Becher told himself as he leaned on the top bar of the corral, watching his men work, and Ruby came up beside him.

Looking off in the direction that Cairew had taken, the girl asked tentatively in a voice so low that it strained Becher's ears, "Are you cross with me, Mel?"

"Why would I be that?" he asked, turning and leaning his back against the rail as he tapped tobacco into a paper.

Reaching out, Ruby took the makings from him, deftly rolled the cigarette, used the tip of a pink tongue to wet the paper, then passed it to him, finished. "We would never have made it, would we, Mel?"

"I doubt it," was his cryptic reply.

Turning, she looked fully at him for the first time since he had returned, her pretty face very sad. "Daddy asked me to wait: said that you would be settling down soon. Is that right?"

Drawing on his cigarette, he delayed answering because he didn't know what to say. Now that they were standing here together, his old feelings for Ruby had largely returned. Apart from his own company, hers was the only one he could relax in. Had things been different, then they would have made a good team. But things would have needed to be very, very different.

"Your daddy is a good man," he told her eventually, not committing himself one way or another.

An astute girl, Ruby knew that he was evading an issue that she so desperately wanted to discuss, but then she faced facts and said, "It's too late now, anyway. I only wish Daddy could get to like Chet some more."

"It's just the age difference," he lied to her. "Your daddy will get to like him."

She was dismissing this with a shake of her head when Zachary came out of the house, spotted them after taking a look around, then walked towards them. Watching her father, judging the distance and the time it would take him to reach them, Ruby seemed to be slightly battling with a decision, then she said, breathlessly, "None of this makes no difference, Chet and me, you know. I may be married, but most of me will always think of you as my man, Mel."

It had taken a lot for the girl to make that statement, and Becher wanted to reach out for her, but couldn't. Her father was close to being within earshot, when Becher said, "Ruby!"

Having turned from him, she looked over her shoulder, and he went on, "I like what you just said to me."

He saw the tears in her eyes, and was glad of the diversion that Zachary's greeting was. In a life that was filled with regrets, Mel Becher came to the conclusion that Ruby Waugh, or whatever her second name was now, was the biggest of them all.

Ruby was still on his mind that afternoon when Ike Stringer rode back in, and Cabel and Pedro joined Cairew at Becher's side as Ike dismounted.

"It's just as you said, Mel," Ike reported, the Adam's apple bobbing in his long neck. He was thin and gangly, unlike his squat, powerfully built brother. "Thursday is when we should hit the bank, and I reckons there'll be more than ten thousand dollars in it. Can't see any problems with it at all. Two men in the street can take care of anything that might happen."

This sounded good, but Becher detected something left unsaid inside of the loosely tied-together figure of Ike Stringer, and he drawled a single-word question at the man, "But?"

A little uncomfortable at having been read so easily, Ike looked at his leader, looked away again, looked back, struggled for words, but failed.

"Speak up, Ike." Caleb Stringer urged his brother, impatiently.

"Well . . . it's just that . . . " Ike tried, and was getting there until Becher's barked command stopped him from speaking further.

"Close it," Becher told him, tapping his own mouth with a forefinger.

Becher's men looked at him uncomprehendingly, but then Chet Wheeler came walking round the side of the house and strolled up to join them, a smile on his young and unhandsome face.

"Howdy, gents," Wheeler said in greeting, sticking his thumbs into his belt.

"You off somewhere, son?" Cairew asked conversationally.

"Nowhere in particular," Chet Wheeler grinned.

"You are now," said Cairew, quietly but menacingly. "Get moving."

Face flushed red, Wheeler seemed to be about to voice a protest, then he turned and did an angrily stiff-legged walk away, and Becher prompted Ike Stringer, "Go ahead, Ike."

"Well," Ike said, having gained confidence during the interlude with Chet Wheeler, "Seems as how Jesse and Frank James got the same kinda idea as we have."

"They in town?" Cairew asked.

"They have been," Ike nodded. "Came in and sized the place up, I heard tell, and they're camped not far away from town now."

"The Youngers with them?" Becher enquired.

"Reckon so, Mel; Clell Miller and Charlie Pitts, too, from what I could gather."

This was news that forced a rethink, and the gang members waited for Becher to say what was to be done. But he walked slowly away from them, and stood looking out along the track that had brought Ike Stringer back — the direction in which Gallatin lay.

Johnny Cairew walked up to Becher, asking quiet-like, "What happens now, Mel?"

"I reckon we ain't going to lose ten thousand dollars," was Becher's reply.

"And the Jameses?"

Becher gave an uncaring shrug as he said, "We'll just have to hit the bank before they do."

7

OLDER folk had an image of the young Sheriff William McDonald fixed in their minds by an incident that summed up what a magnificent fighting-man he had once been. This had taken place in the incorrectly named Straight Chance Saloon, when a tough straight off the trail had taunted McDonald, claiming that he wouldn't be such a big man unarmed, and inviting him to take off his gunbelt and settle matters with his fists. Perfectly capable of downing a man twice his size, the sheriff had checked to see that the man wore no gunbelt, and had then unbuckled his and laid it on the bar. When McDonald turned he found himself looking into the muzzle of a .38 the man had carried concealed inside of his shirt. Enraged by the cheat, the sheriff had leapt upon him, knocking the gun from his hand before the man had chance to use it, then breaking his assailant's back with a crack that had forever lived on in the minds of those who had heard it.

But people these days knew another, older McDonald, a little slower in his movements, but still a dedicated lawman, renowned for his patience and attention to detail. To him a crime was a crime, whether it was the robbing of a stage with the shooting of the driver and shotgun rider, or the theft of a few beef, such as had been happening on Geoffrey Barker's Circle M ranch of late, and which had kept McDonald and two temporary deputies, Jim Chole and Abe Swetner, sitting out on the range for two days and two nights.

But though McDonald's kind of policing was effective, it was also expensive, and he was aware that public funds wouldn't stretch to him keeping his two helpers out here for the third night that was coming up. After all, the end result would probably be the arrest of two or three cow-punchers living on the outer edge of lawlessness by stealing a few cows and making some extra dollars.

Funnily enough, when he had sent Chole and Abe Swetner back to town, McDonald had his first piece of luck by coming upon about twenty head of cattle, all bearing the Circle M brand, holed up in a blind canyon to the east of Barker's spread.

Settling down, a blanket round him, his back against a rock, Sheriff McDonald had nothing to do but wait — and that was something he was real good at. If it took a week or a month, the rustlers would come here either to add to their stolen herd or move it away for a sale, and the sheriff would be waiting.

He didn't, in fact, have any longer than dusk to wait. First he heard cattle approaching, and the way the beef he was watching raised their heads confirmed for him that his ears had heard aright. Shedding the blanket in movements as natural as a snake dropping its skin, McDonald, who had moved his horse off aways so that it could make no sound that would alarm the rustlers, took up his chosen position at the side of a large rock.

From where he waited he saw them coming; ten head of beef being pushed along by two men who rode easily, slowly, and unsuspectingly in their saddles. Letting the cattle pass him by, McDonald then stepped out, rifle at the ready as he shouted his command.

"Hold it, right there."

Hearing his own voice echoing around the canyon, the sheriff covered the two men, who were just silhouettes in the twilight. But one of the figures moved, drawing a gun as it wheeled its horse, but a shot from McDonald sent the man flying out of the saddle to go crashing to the ground, spooking his horse as he did so, causing it to squeal shrilly and then gallop off wildly as the sheriff swung his rifle to cover the second man.

"Don't shoot, Sheriff," the rider cried in panic, raising his arms high, and the sheriff recognized the high voice of Chet Wheeler.

"Get down from that horse, you danged fool of a kid," McDonald told the boy, who obeyed as the sheriff walked to the body of the man he had shot, turning it on to its back with his foot, looking down into the sightless eyes and blood-gushing mouth of another youngster whom he recognized, and he said with sadness, "Bill Ryall."

McDonald had seen this kid the first day he had ridden into town, a drifter with no prospects until Geoff Barker had taken him on. Here was the rancher's repayment for his kindness — having his cattle thieved. Who led whom, the sheriff wondered — was Wheeler the one who had thought up the rustling, and Ryall the weaker of the two who had been persuaded to join, or maybe it was the other way around. Not that it mattered a damn now, the part Ryall had played was definitely at an end, which probably meant that Chet Wheeler, who was left to face the music, was the unluckiest of the pair.

Going to Wheeler, who was trembling, his hands still held high, McDonald pulled the youngster's arms down and tied them behind his back, leaving a length of rope dangling. Then he tethered the boy's horse to a parched, dying tree, before knotting the loose end of the rope about the wrists of Wheeler to the horn of his saddle. Deliberately pulling the rope tight, the sheriff had Wheeler, whose back was jammed against his horse, standing painfully on his toes, stretched up by the arms.

"Is Billy dead?" Wheeler quavered.

Ignoring the question, McDonald's movements were positive as he led Ryall's horse to the body, then lifted up the dead boy and draped him over the saddle. The horse shied at the smell of blood, and when it settled down, the sheriff secured the body with rope.

In no hurry to be moving, as he intended to drive the stolen cattle back to the ranch on his way back to town, McDonald lit a fire and squatted by it to boil coffee and drink it, totally oblivious to the begging, pleading noises that Wheeler made throughout.

Tipping the last of the coffee on to the fire, savouring the aroma of the smoke, the sheriff eased out his legs after having hunkered for so long, then walked to his captive to untie him from the saddle horn, half toss him up on to his horse before leading Ryall's horse over and securing its reins to the back of Wheeler's saddle.

Freeing the reins of Wheeler's horse from the tree, McDonald led both animals over to his own horse, mounted up, and rode out with them behind him, calling softly to the cattle as he moved in behind them, shifting them out of the box canyon.

They rode through the night in silence, the closeness of his friend's corpse seeming to unnerve Chet Wheeler, and what sounded like crying had reached the sheriff's ears. Unheeding, he plodded on the cattle in front of him, altering the pace of his horse only when the small herd picked up the scent of water ahead and broke into a shambling run.

Letting the cattle drink at the creek, and refreshing the three horses, McDonald, sitting as still and quiet as a totem pole, slowly turned his head in Wheeler's direction as the man called him.

"Does Ruby have to know about this?"

"I reckon as how she'll guess," the sheriff drawled sarcastically, "when I lock you up in jail on a rustling charge. She's bound to notice when you don't go home."

"She don't deserve this," Wheeler moaned.

"To my way of reckoning she didn't deserve a crittur like you, Wheeler."

"What about Zachary Waugh!" a

sudden, frightening thought came to Wheeler. "He'll nail my hide to a fence post."

McDonald grinned through the darkness at the distraught boy. "I sure reckon that's what old Zach will want to do to you, son, but he ain't going to get the chance — 'cos I'm going to do it."

With the animals watered, the sheriff jerked the reins of Wheeler's horse and they were moving again, the cattle occasionally lowing their pleasure into the night, totally refreshed by the water. They rode on until they topped a ridge in the false dawn and there, minute in the far distance, they could see the Circle M ranch. That was when Chet Wheeler began to beg.

"You could give me another chance, Sheriff. I ain't never done nothing wrong before."

Without even turning his head, McDonald told him, "Let Billy Ryall take the blame, it that what you mean?"

"It ain't going to make no difference

to Billy now," Wheeler pointed out, selfishly.

"Billy's well out of it," the sheriff commented in disgust. "I sure wouldn't want a cur like you for a partner."

Discouraged, although reluctant to accept the worst, Wheeler stayed quiet for several miles, then he called out, and was pleased when he saw his words jerk the body of the sheriff.

"You know a real mean *hombre* named Becher, Sheriff?"

After the initial shock of hearing this, McDonald recovered himself and rode on for a while without answering. Then he tossed the words carelessly into the air for Wheeler to catch, "What if I do?"

"Thought you might be interested that him and his gang are staying at Zachary's place."

Reining in his horse, McDonald turned in his saddle. "You feeding me lies, sonny?"

"No, sir," Wheeler said enthusiastically, delighted that he had the sheriff interested. "He's a friend of Zachary's. Takes too much notice of Ruby for my liking."

"Is he on his own?" the sheriff tested the boy.

"Doggone it, he sure ain't." Wheeler made the most of having the attention of the sheriff. "There's five of them altogether — some kind of half-breed by the name of Cairew, two brothers, Ike and Cabel something, I don't know their second name, and a greaser."

Dismounting, McDonald walked back to stand beside Wheeler's horse and look up at the boy, his face serious. "What are they doing in these parts, boy?"

"I don't rightly know, sir, but I sure could find out."

Not answering, the sheriff stared up at the young man for some time, neither his expression nor his eyes betraying his thoughts, then, without a word he turned on his heel, went back to his horse, mounted up and started moving once more.

Half an hour later, when the real dawn showed them how close they were to the ranch house of the Circle M, McDonald again stopped and went back to speak to Wheeler. This time they conversed for quite a while, and there was a smile on Wheeler's weak face when the sheriff drew a knife and cut him free, and untied the reins of Ryall's horse from the saddle.

As Wheeler rubbed his wrists, grimacing in pain as the blood circulation started up in full, McDonald poked out a warning forefinger of a massive hand at him as he said, "Let me down, son, and nothing'll save you."

"You can rely on me, Sheriff," Chet Wheeler promised as he rode off in the direction of Zachary Waugh's homestead.

Sheriff William McDonald watched the young man go. Standing there in the golden sun of a new day, his indecision registered on his craggy face, as he wondered on whether he had done the right thing. He saw the rider diminish in size as the distance between them increased. He watched Wheeler go over a hill that took him from his sight, and the sheriff made a silent vow that would have struck terror into the heart of Chet Wheeler had he knowledge of it.

Then McDonald mounted up, driving his little herd of cows, leading the horse that carried the body of the man he had killed.

8

"WE are a fast-growing town," Levi Brandt told them proudly.

With the awkwardness of strangers at a large gathering of folk who knew each other well, Rita Martin and Iain Fulton were grateful to the store owner for making it easier on them. In surroundings to which he was well suited, Iain, who had been uncomfortable during the long train journey, and well out of his depth riding the trail with the outlaw band, had become his former, poised self, but Rita was finding it difficult to adapt to this new town which was, naturally, full of people she didn't know.

Elizabeth Brandt leaned her silver-haired, elegant head close to Rita so as to be heard above the orchestra. "And we're delighted to have you both here.

New, young blood, that's what Gallatin needs more than anything right now."

"Indeed," her husband agreed, wishing he had thought of expressing that greeting and sentiment, and making up for it with a beaming smile shared between Rita and Iain. "We have these little evenings once a month now. It gives the business people of the town a chance for discussion in a social atmosphere."

A number of people were dancing. The band expertly played 'Greensleeves' but for Rita there was none of the magic in that tune that she had found, and now wouldn't leave her, in the harmonica playing out in the wilds on a dark night. That experience seemed to have brought out a wildness in her that even she hadn't known existed.

"Am I right in believing that we should be congratulating both of you?" the regal Mrs Brandt was asking.

Rita nodded, for she, having seen the impossibility of the life of adventure that she'd had a sudden yen for, had agreed to marry Iain. With a house of their own, and her mother coming out West to live with them, she hoped that everything would settle down and revert to what she had accepted as her life before the train she'd been riding on had been held up.

"Five weeks time," Iain told Elizabeth Brandt, whose husband shook him warmly by the hand.

"You are indeed a lucky man," Brandt remarked. "Having such a responsible position at the bank while still so young, and such a lovely bride."

"Thank you," a blushing Rita said.

"Do you know," Mrs Brandt mused, "that yours, to the best of my recollection, will be the first wedding in Gallatin in the four years that we've been here."

"That's not surprising," her husband cynically put in. "The only other young women coming to town find work in Betty Banham's establishment, a place where the sacrament of marriage is abused rather than used."

With a little shudder, Mrs Brandt complained, "Do we have to mention that terrible place!"

"Somebody talking about the bank again?" a joking Peter Welman, the young owner of the Gallatin hauliers and owner of the stage that ran regularly to the nearest railhead, joined them. Both Rita and Iain had met Welman before, and each of them liked his bright and breezy manner.

"Without the bank, young Peter," Brandt reminded the newcomer, "you might well still be driving a team for old Percy Smallman."

"And you wouldn't have my custom at your store," Welman retorted jovially.

This made Brandt laugh and turn to Iain. "There, you see how important your bank is to all of us."

It was all good, friendly stuff, and Iain commented on it later while Rita and he were dancing. "We've certainly been made welcome. I was worried that the townsfolk might be somewhat insular."

"I'm glad that they're not," Rita replied, feeling better now as she let her body move to the rhythm of the music.

In a way there was a satisfaction to being an essential part of a thriving, growing town, albeit her role being a proxy one. As Iain's fiancée the attention she was getting this evening would, Rita was fully aware, register as nothing compared to the regard she would be held in as his wife. Iain's position made him a powerful man indeed in this area, and, in a routine that had been part of the evening so far, Levi Brandt was waiting yet again to introduce them to someone else.

This time it was a tall, moustachioed man with a craggy, unsmiling face, and the build of a prizefighter, whose light-blue eyes fixed on them, holding them both in a penetrating gaze, as Brandt ushered them up to shake hands.

"Sheriff, may I introduce Miss Rita Martin, and her intended, Mr Iain Fulton, who is the new man in charge of the bank here," Brandt made the introductions. "Miss Martin, Mr Fulton, this is Sheriff William McDonald."

They shook hands, Rita losing her tiny one in the shovel-like hand of the sheriff, while Peter Welman, who was standing beside the smiling Brandt, cracked, "When you get around to fiddling the books, Iain, this is the man who'll be locking you up in the local hoosegow."

There was no smile on McDonald's face, but his brow was creased in puzzlement as he repeated Rita's name to himself. "Martin? Martin? Martin?" Then the memory he had been wracking his brains for came to him. "Begging your pardon, miss, but are you any kin to Silas Martin who was gunned down in a bank robbery over in Adair County?"

Iain reached for Rita's hand as her face clouded and she told the sheriff, "I was. He was my father, Sheriff."

"I'm sorry, miss." The sheriff toyed

uncomfortably with the stetson he held in both hands. "Bad business that. That's Saul Belling's territory, but I heard tell all about it. It was the James boys by all accounts."

"I'm sorry for Miss Martin, but do we have to talk about things that will spoil the evening for everyone, Sheriff?" Elizabeth Brandt protested.

Ignoring her, Welman said to McDonald, "I've heard a rumour that Jesse James has been seen around here."

The small gathering went quiet at this, and the playing orchestra faded into a distance for Rita. A picture ran through her mind of the men who had rode slowly by when she had been looking out of the window of the bank.

"Surely not," Levi Brandt snorted his scorn, but Rita could have confirmed what Peter Welman had said, because she was now without doubt that she had looked into the eyes of the infamous Jesse James.

"What would the James gang want in a town like ours?" Elizabeth Brandt echoed her husband's disbelief.

Bending his head to Iain, the sheriff said quietly, "That is something I'd like to discuss with you, Mr Fulton."

With a hand on his elbow, McDonald moved Iain away from the group. Welman went with the two of them, but when Rita went to join her fiancé, both he and the sheriff gestured for her to stay where she was.

McDonald said gravely, "This concerns you mostly, but it could include you and your stage, Pete. I ain't sure about the James boys, that could be no more than rumour, but I reckon on how one gang is lying low close to Gallatin."

"The bank?" a worried Iain gasped.

"Reckon that's about the cut of it, son," the sheriff said. "These boys hit banks, railroads, and stage-lines. Like as how you've met them already, Mr Fulton."

A white-faced Iain realized what the

sheriff meant. "The men who robbed the train!"

"That's them," the sheriff agreed. "Mel Becher and his gang."

"You got me worried now," Peter Welman put in. "I didn't reckon I was big enough to interest Jesse James, but Becher is different."

Noticing that Rita was staring at him, concern on her face, Iain tried to give her what he hoped was a reassuring smile. He didn't like what he was hearing. With Rita agreeing to marry him, and with his finding his new position at the bank easier to fill than he had ever anticipated, life had been idyllic — but now!

"Trouble is, son," McDonald was unhappily telling him, "I gotta be away from town over the next few days. I'll have my deputies keep an eye on the bank, of course, but I won't be here to back you up."

Something that had the feel of icy water began to trickle down Iain Fulton's spine, and his scalp was going prickly, as if every hair was standing up on his head, individually and at intervals. He stammered, "What can I do, Sheriff?"

"If it's Jesse James, run like mad," Welman said unhelpfully.

"Like I said," the sheriff told Iain, "I'll have my deputies make a point of watching the bank. Anyway, I'll be back in a couple of days: three at the most."

It was a gloomy Iain who walked back to Rita. He'd heard of the James gang, of course, but they were remote to him, like reading the stories of outlaws in those penny publications they got back East. It was different with Becher. Though he was ashamed to admit it to himself, throughout the short time he had spent with Becher, he had been terrified of the man.

"What on earth's the matter?" Rita asked, scanning his face anxiously.

"Nothing to worry about," he tried to reassure her, but his voice cracked.

"What did the sheriff tell you?" she

insisted, but he was saved by the Brandts and some other people who came up to pull them into a 'Paul' Jones.

As he whirled in the dance, changing partners, swinging on the arms of different women, exchanging the tentative smiles of strangers, Iain was able to get things better into perspective. The immensity of what McDonald had cautioned about seemed to shrink. As Levi Brandt had pointed out earlier, this was a big town. The bank was on a busy street that was lined by other businesses. There would be plenty of people to come to the aid of the bank in an emergency.

He voiced this theory to Rita when the evening had ended and he was walking her back to Mrs Costain's, but she wasn't impressed.

"The folk we were with tonight won't be able to help you, Iain," she stressed. "They would be no match for somebody like Jesse James, and it would be wrong to expect them to try."

They were in the respectable part of town now, with women passing on the arms of their men, but the noise from the saloon area was a reminder of how tough things really were. He wondered how much of what the sheriff had said he should tell Rita, and decided that it was wrong to keep anything from her.

"Sheriff McDonald doesn't seem to think there is any danger from the Jameses, but he says that Mel Becher and his men are somewhere nearby."

Feeling a little giddy as she heard the name, Rita rested her fingers on Iain's forearm to steady herself. It couldn't be coincidence: Mel Becher had known they were heading for Gallatin, although he couldn't have had any idea what for. Was she, Rita wondered, haunting the outlaw like he had been living in her mind since their unusual meeting? If so, that was what had brought him to this town. The sheriff and Iain were reading it wrong.

"I don't think the bank is in any

danger from Mel Becher," she told them when they stood outside of the house in which she had a room.

In the flickering lights of an occasional flare from the odd lamps that were dotted about the street, Iain looked very young, and more than a little frightened. A terrible doubt, amounting to almost an ominous premonition, rose in her at the thought that this was the man she was to marry in a few weeks.

"I wish I could share your confidence," he told her earnestly as he turned to leave.

Alone in her room, with sleep far away and the future frighteningly near, Rita prayed for guidance. If the gang leader was here at Gallatin because of her, then it would be foolish to even contemplate a life with him, riding between robberies, being chased by sheriffs and their men.

Yet wouldn't it perhaps be even more foolish to marry Iain Fulton, a young man who had nothing in him to match what Rita knew she had within herself? What a choice, she thought miserably — die by the gun or out of boredom!

Dawn was lightening the gloom of her room before her eyelids began to droop, and even then she slept very little.

9

THEY split up to ride into Gallatin, with Becher and Cairew riding together up front, and the Stringers and Pedro following at intervals. It was early afternoon on a breezeless day so hot that the trail to town shimmered in front of them as their horses paced slowly, the riders wanting to appear unhurried, unworried, inconspicuous. When the outskirts of the town came into view, Cairew broke the silence between himself and his leader.

"I don't like that kid back there knowing so much," he said.

Turning his head, Becher looked steadily at him. "If he went to Jesse James they'd blow him out of the saddle before he got within talking distance, Johnny."

"I ain't thinking about him going to the Jameses."

121

"The sheriff!" Becher grasped what his deputy meant. "You reckon as how my feelings towards Ruby are going to get us gunned down, Johnny?"

"I didn't say that, Mel," Cairew argued, "and I'd never get around to thinking it. You can always be relied on. But that kid makes me uneasy."

Though he wouldn't admit it to Cairew, Chet Wheeler worried him, too. It was obvious that the kid was jealous of him and resented Becher being at the homestead. Ruby's choice of a partner would forever remain beyond the understanding of Becher, but the effect it had on him and his plans was plain to see, and it was what Cairew was talking about now. Zachary Waugh had always been totally trustworthy, and his daughter's loyalty could never be doubted, but Chet Wheeler was someone Becher would rather not have in his life.

"Problem is, Johnny," he told Cairew as they rode, "that like it or not, that boy is Zach's son-in-law, which is something Zach don't take too kindly to himself. I can't push the kid away without upsetting Zach. That don't mean to say that I ain't watching Wheeler all the time."

"And if he steps out of line?"

"I'll kill him," Becher replied softly and evenly.

"That's what I figured," a satisfied Cairew breathed out in relief, and they didn't speak again as they covered the final distance into town.

As planned, Becher and Cairew rode down to the centre of the street, dismounting and hitching their horses to a rail outside of a general store. The other three would pull up separately at different vantage points, working out the best escape routes. Looking for places of possible ambush if the law should learn their plans.

With the bank just three buildings away, Becher and Cairew averted suspicion by entering the store. A silver-haired woman was behind the large counter to their left, a position that seemed beneath her, while a man advanced on them, smiling, right hand outstretched.

"Welcome to Gallatin, gentlemen. A good town to be in if you're fixing to stay."

Both shook hands with him briefly, then Becher looked around the store with the air of a prospective customer, as Cairew told the storekeeper, "Just passing through, mister."

"So be it," the storekeeper sighed, as if the chief desire was to have Becher and Cairew settle in town. "Well, just state your pleasure, gentlemen, and my good lady will attend to your needs. Elizabeth!"

Becher bought some tobacco from the woman, and Cairew was purchasing a box of .45 shells, as Becher turned away from the counter. The storekeeper was busy shifting full sacks around at the far end, and there was no one else in the place until a woman came in through the open door. Averting his face, not wanting too many in this town to identify him, just in case, Becher made the movement slow so that it looked natural, and that was how he slipped up.

He heard a little gasping sigh from the woman customer, and brought his head back to her. Mel Becher and Rita Martin found themselves facing each other, the shock of the meeting opening her eyes wide in her beautiful face. Raising his hand, not sure what signal he was thinking of making, Becher saw that Rita was fast recovering her mental balance, and he put his forefinger to his mouth in cautioning gesture.

But she turned and fled from the store in such haste that the woman behind the counter looked questioningly from Becher to Cairew, who drawled, "Changed her mind, I guess."

The woman smiled, far from convinced, as Cairew picked up his change from the counter before joining Becher in a walk to the door, the storekeeper calling out behind them,

"Any time, gentlemen."

"A pleasure doing business with you," Cairew said as they went out into the street, and there was amusement in his dark eyes as he observed Becher look to his left then his right.

"Lost something, Mel?" he grinned.

Aware that Johnny's sharp eyes and powers of observation couldn't be fooled, Becher said, "You saw who she was."

"Sure did," Cairew nodded, "but I don't reckon as how she'll cause us any trouble, seeing as how she helped you out with the posse that time."

"I wasn't thinking that," Becher said morosely and there were no words he knew of to tell Cairew just what he was thinking, and if there had been he wouldn't have done so.

They were standing on the boardwalk, turning in the direction of the bank, when Ike Stringer walked past, not looking at them but speaking out of the corner of his mouth. "We were tailed into town. One man."

As they walked, Cairew asked, "Wheeler?" and Becher nodded, replying bitterly, "Who else!"

There were two tellers at work in the bank when they entered, one busy with a woman customer and the other completing what had the look of an involved cash transaction with a man who had the appearance of a merchant. Becher went to a table on which some literature had been laid out, and sat in a chair, surreptitiously studying a leaflet while his eyes took in the whole area. To his right, an observant Cairew was standing at something like a lectern, counting notes as if he was about to deposit money, innocent enough to the casual observer, but Becher was aware that his right-hand man's mind was registering everything around him.

Having feared that the unexpected encounter with Rita Martin would make if difficult for him to concentrate, Becher was pleased to discover that he was his old cool, calculating self. Two elderly men came into the bank together to stand talking to the left of both Becher and Cairew. At the other side of them, a door to a back room opened and a cattleman came out, with a young man, immaculately dressed, obviously the bank's executive, who stepped out behind the customer, shook hands with him in farewell, and went back in, closing the door behind him.

It all made sense to Becher now, mind-numbing sense, explaining the presence of Rita Martin in Gallatin. He looked quickly in the direction of Cairew, but could tell that he hadn't spotted Fulton because the two elderly men had blocked his view. Becher didn't mention his discovery to Cairew when they left the bank together, and neither did he say anything about it when they rode out of town, confident that the other three members of the gang would be following, spaced out, each one carrying separate but vital information.

They had covered about a third of the distance back to the Waugh homestead, and were passing some high bluffs on their right, when there came the angry, echoing crack of a rifle, and a bullet ploughed into the dust in front of them, causing both horses to rear.

When they had the animals under control, they saw that a man had stepped out from between some high brush, his hands out from his side, ready to draw if necessary, but his gun still in its holster. There was no way that he could have fired the rifle shot, and while keeping him under surveillance covertly, both Becher and Cairew scanned the bluffs, unsuccessfully seeking the rifleman.

"You got it," the man standing in front of them said. "You're both covered. Make one wrong move and you're dead."

Recognition brought Cairew's face alive. "William Stiles."

"They calls me Clell Miller now, Cairew," the man corrected him, before adding, "Jesse wants a word."

Another man stepped out on to the

trail, and Becher, for the first time in more than a decade, found himself face to face with Jesse James. The face was harder, a few more lines had been added, but otherwise Jesse was as handsome and slim as ever.

"It's been a long time, Mel," Jesse James said in a quiet voice, getting nothing more than a nod in return from Becher. He turned his gaze on to Cairew. "And you're Johnny Cairew!"

"That's me," Cairew acknowledged, but Jesse had lost interest in him.

"It ain't kind of social-like, Mel, not dismounting when you meet an old friend," Jesse James complained.

"Old friends don't shoot at each other," Becher rejoined, causing a smile to flit across James's face.

"That's because I respect you as a fighting man, Mel. If I'd just ridden up on you, then you'd have plugged me dead centre before I got a word out. I hear that your man, Cairew, can handle himself too."

Getting down from his horse, with

Cairew doing the same, Becher used the movement as a cover for a glance behind to check if the Stringers and Pedro were riding up, all unsuspecting. But Jesse James was sharp, and he managed another smile as he informed Becher, "Your men will be delayed, Mel, but only until we've had our little chat."

"What do we have to chat about, Jesse?"

"A mutual interest."

"Which is?"

Jesse James shook his good-looking head in mild disgust. "Don't try to joss me, Mel. You know we're talking of the bank in Gallatin."

"Now that," Becher drawled, "is a subject on which I ain't yet made up my mind, Jesse."

Shifting his slim body in a way that warned both Becher and Cairew that he was preparing to draw on them, Jesse James spoke menacingly as Miller also altered his stance. "Then I guess I'll have to make up your mind for you,

Becher, right now."

James had made a mistake in not noticing that when Becher and Cairew had got down from their saddles they had put their horses between themselves and the rifleman up in the bluffs. If Jesse James was relying on back-up from there, then he was out of luck.

There was no need for an audible or visual signal to pass between Becher and Cairew, who knew each other's moves well after many years spent together. By a split second they beat both James and Miller to the draw, and both of those men, eyes wide as they stared the likelihood of death in the face, threw themselves to one side. Too late, Jesse James had recognized that he could expect no help from the man with the rifle.

Not firing their guns, Becher and Cairew leapt up on to their horses, kicking the spurs in and leaping away. Jesse James and his man had no chance to get off a shot, and the man with the rifle had to hold his fire lest he hit one of them. Becher and Cairew had travelled a fair distance before a rifle slug whistled past them, and then they were too far along the trail for the sharpshooter to be any threat to them.

When they were well clear, but still keeping their horses at a gallop, Cairew shouted across to Becher, "What do you reckon with Pedro and the Stringers?"

"I listened," Becher shouted back, "but didn't hear any shots."

"Neither did I," Cairew agreed.

When they arrived back at the Waugh homestead, they put their horses in the lean-to at the back of the house, and feared the worst when they saw that the horses of Ike, Cabel and Pedro were not there.

"Do you reckon they ran into the Youngers?" Cairew asked worriedly.

"Reckon so," Becher nodded gravely. As good as his three men were, they were not up to taking on formidable gunmen like Cole, Jim, and Bob

Younger, all three of whom had distinguished themselves in war, and were now greatly feared as outlaws in peace.

Walking over to where Chet Wheeler's horse stood, Becher thought he saw a light haze of steam rising from the animal, and that the horse had been recently ridden was confirmed when he ran his hand around its neck and down its back.

"Well?" Cairew enquired from the other end of the lean-to.

"He ain't been back here long," Becher told him.

"He could be in with Jesse," suggested Cairew.

"I'll know before long," Becher promised grimly as they walked into the house.

The three occupants of the room looked up as Becher and Cairew came in, Ruby, who was sewing patches on to a shirt for her father, having a special smile for Becher. Zachary himself was oiling a rifle, and he greeted the pair of them with a question about the absent trio.

"Saw you both ride in, Mel. Where's Pedro and the Stringers?"

"They'll be along shortly," Cairew said, though neither Becher nor himself really believed it.

From where he bent over at the task of repairing a set of harness, Chet Wheeler didn't speak or look up, but he must have felt Mel Becher's eyes boring into him. Ruby noticed it, and she looked both upset and afraid.

10

"**Y**OU beat Jesse James to the draw?" Pedro said with glee before his laugh split the late evening air.

The five of them were standing at the back of the house, Pedro and the Stringers having recently ridden in to relate how they had, while on the trail from town, spotted someone in wait, and all three had made a long detour back to the Waugh place. They didn't know, until Becher and Cairew told them, that they had escaped a run-in with the Youngers.

"Mel did, I didn't," Cairew put Pedro right. "I was fronting a mean *hombre* I knew as William Stiles, but he reckons his name is Clell Miller now."

Cabel Stringer had concern for Becher in his eyes as he warned,

"Jesse ain't going to take kindly to being beat, Mel."

Shrugging, Becher rolled himself a cigarette, then passed the makings to Cairew. Nobody spoke, the only sound being the mournful cry of a night bird, until both men had lit up, then Pedro commented, "Kinda complicates things, don't it, having the James boys after the same bank?" There was regret on his dark face as he went on, "Pity, it would have been easy."

"Still will be," Cairew told him confidently. "You heard Mel say the Jameses won't keep us away from that sort of money."

He was looking at Becher for confirmation that wasn't forthcoming. The gang leader seemed preoccupied. Then Becher suddenly leapt round to the side of the house. There was scuffling and a muttered curse, and the other four members of the gang followed Becher, arriving to see him throwing a man through the air. The figure landed in the dust at the front of the house, rolling over and raising itself up, and they could see in the half-light that it was Chet Wheeler.

The blow that had sent the youngster on to his back must have been a powerful one, and Wheeler was shaking his head now, trying to clear it, with Becher standing a little way off, looking down on him.

There was a blur of action then that was illuminated by the light of an oil lamp spilling out into the night as Ruby, alarmed by the noises outside, opened the door of the house. Chet Wheeler was pulling his gun from his holster, but before the barrel could clear leather, the .45 of Becher had been drawn and was levelled at him. Seeing this, Ruby screamed and ran towards her young husband, who released a shot at Becher, who had been rendered helpless by the proximity of Ruby to Wheeler. He couldn't risk a shot.

A slug from Wheeler's gun ripped through the material of Becher's shirt, grazing his left shoulder as it did so, and he could feel the warm trickling of blood down his arm. But Becher had no time to be occupied by a minor injury. Pushing his wife a little to one side, Chet Wheeler, still sitting in the dirt, was aiming his gun at Becher once more. In one flowing movement that was accompanied by a frightened scream from Ruby, Becher leapt forwards, a kick from him sending the .44 flying from Wheeler's hand while, as his own momentum carried him by, Becher brought the barrel of his .45 down on Chet Wheeler's skull.

The other men came hurrying up as Ruby knelt cradling her husband's split-open head, which was gushing blood.

"Carry the kid into the house," Becher ordered, and the Stringers bent to pick up Wheeler as their leader walked off into the darkness.

Neither had Becher come back when they carried Wheeler to his bed, where Ruby bathed and bandaged the damaged head. Looking up as the men came back into the rooms, Zachary Waugh asked, "Well?"

"He'll live," Pedro told the older man, joining the Stringers in surprise as they were gestured into seats, and their host prepared to pour drinks for them all. This was the first time that any of them but Cairew had been in the house.

"I don't mean the Wheeler kid," Zachary Waugh snapped. "Who gives a darn about what happens to that crittur?"

"Your daughter does," Cairew reminded him gently.

"More fool her." Zachary had lost patience with Ruby and her man. "I wanna know what's going on."

"The James' gang is around; Jesse's interested in the bank at Gallatin," Cairew said.

"Ah!" Understanding dawned on Zachary. "They've heard tell of the big money." He was thoughtful for a moment. "Where does the boy fit into this? I ain't never known Mel Becher whup nobody without good reason, and he sure beat up on that boy."

Selecting his words, wanting to be as kind as possible, Cairew told him. "Reckon as how the boy's been spying on us, Zach."

"Never!" Zachary Waugh exploded, not in disbelief but disgust. "You reckon he's sided with the Jameses? Nah! That can't be so! Jesse James wouldn't never have nothing to do with a cur like Chet Wheeler."

"My reckoning is," Johnny Cairew said calmly, "that the kid is after the price on Becher's head."

Zachary was furious. "If that's so, I'll kill the son-of-a-bitch."

"If that's so, Mel Becher will kill the son-of-a-bitch," said Cairew sardonically.

★ ★ ★

Quite by chance, Sheriff William McDonald had come across Deputy Marshal Larren Peake at a trading post

141

while on his way back to Gallatin. They took a drink together, necessity forcing McDonald to endure the company of Peake, an unpleasant man whose overt slyness was emphasized by his unfortunate cross-eyes. Peake, who didn't state his business to the sheriff, had twenty men with him, all armed to the teeth. Across the table from Peake in a corner of the post, McDonald lifted the third drink he had paid for, Peake yet to offer to pay for one, and told the deputy marshal what he thought was about to happen at Gallatin.

Peake laughed in his face, his long yellow teeth each with a black band where they joined the gums. "The James boys and Becher's gang, you say, Sheriff? My, my, why don't you add the Daltons for good measure?"

Fighting to control the anger rising in him, McDonald remained quiet for a time, aware that he needed Peake and his men. With what he had to support him back at Gallatin, the sheriff couldn't have braced either of the gangs, let alone both together. Why Becher had teamed up with the Jameses he couldn't guess. Mel Becher was a loner apart from the men who had ridden with him for years. Both gangs, that of Jesse James and Becher, were feared, but not hated in the way the Daltons, whom Peake had just mentioned, were. There was nothing vicious — not vicious in the sense of using violence for the sake of violence — in either of the gangs. That didn't mean, of course, that they didn't present a danger to every lawman in the territory.

"I'm a busy man, McDonald," Peake said, raising his glass to his lips.

"Too busy to nab the James boys and Mel Becher's gang?" the sheriff tempted him, and was rewarded by the sight of Peake closing his out-of-track eyes in order to think.

Finishing his drink, making it obvious that he expected another, Larren Peake stood and walked over to stand at the window looking out at his men. The waiting McDonald refilled his own glass, then, as Peake turned and slowly made his way back to the table, he poured another drink for the deputy marshal.

Sitting, Peake looked over his glass in his cross-eyed way at McDonald. "I'll ride with you, but let me warn you, McDonald, that if we're going to end up chasing shadows, then I'll sure take it out of your hide."

Jumping to his feet, McDonald reached both hands across the table to grab the deputy marshal by the lapels of his coat and yank him violently upright, knocking the table sideways, sending glasses, a bottle, and drink to the floor. At the far end of the room, the alarmed agent of the post was in a dilemma, wondering whether to call Peake's men in.

With his face close to Peake's ugly, unshaven one, McDonald ground out his words. "To threaten me one time is once too many, Peake."

"Hold on there, pardner," the deputy

marshal tried to ease the situation he was in. "I'll ride with you, sure enough, and we'll get those renegades together."

Shaking his head, McDonald put it right. "You'll ride with me, Peake, but *I'll* be giving the orders all along the line, savvy?"

"We'll do it your way," Peake conceded, the bravado chased out of him, and needing to cling to the edge of the capsized table for support when McDonald released him.

"Now we understand each other," a contented sheriff said. "Get your men mounted as soon as you can, Peake."

★ ★ ★

To three of them it sounded like a retreat in the face of Jesse James, with only Cairew recognizing that Becher must have another reason. Pedro checked for the sake of himself and the Stringers. "We do not hit the bank at Gallatin, Señor Becher?"

Becher nodded, an apology in his eyes as he looked straight at the Mexican. "There'll be other towns, other banks, Pedro."

"Then let's go saddle up," Ike Stringer said, making for the door, followed by his brother and Pedro, watched unhappily by Zachary Waugh. But the three men stopped when they noticed that Cairew had made no move. Being more intelligent than them, and knowing Becher better than they did, Johnny Cairew was waiting for more from Becher, and he wasn't wrong.

"You riding out tonight, Mel?" Zachary enquired apprehensively, not wanting to lose his friend for another indeterminable period.

"No, we're not finished in Gallatin yet," Becher told him, and his three men who had been ready to leave came back to stand waiting to hear what he had to say.

"If we ain't hitting the bank, the Jameses will, so what's left here for us?" Cabel Stringer wanted to know.

146

Delaying an answer, the normally taciturn Becher then made what was for him a speech. "At all other times I have expected you to follow me in whatever we have done, but this is different. This time, if any or all of you want to stay out of it, then that's up to you, and I won't bear a grudge. We can work together again afterwards."

"I don't get it, Mel." Ike Stringer's face showed that he was bewildered. "What have you got in mind?"

"There's no law to speak of in Gallatin right now . . . " Becher began, to be involuntarily interrupted by Zachary Waugh.

"That's what I told ya! Will McDonald had business away from town, which makes it the right time for a bank raid," Zachary protested.

"That's not what I'm looking at," Becher said, then gave them all a shock by continuing, "What I intend to do is stop the James boys from hitting the bank. Anyone who wants to join me is welcome, but, like I said, if you want to stay out of this one, then there'll be no hard feelings."

"Us on the side of the law?" Cabel Stringer couldn't believe what he had heard. "Doggone it, Mel, you cain't be thinking straight."

"I have my reasons," was all Becher would say, but he could tell that only Cairew understood what those reasons were. "Take a while to think about it."

Walking out of the house, Becher stood on the verandah. He was staring into the blackness of the night in which he tried to read his own thoughts, when Cairew came out in his silent way to stand beside him.

"I'll be with you in Gallatin," Cairew said.

"You don't have to be, Johnny," a grateful Becher told him.

Shrugging, Cairew gave a little grin. "I'm not sure of that. We been together so long, Mel, that I ain't sure that I can operate without you."

"You could try if you wanted to."

Becher kept his reply as light as possible.

"I guess I don't want to," Cairew told him in his low-voiced way.

Over there was Gallatin, Becher told himself, where the beautiful Rita Martin was probably asleep right now. She had to become one of the few, but profound, forgotten dreams in his life. The gulf between their different ways of life couldn't be crossed for them ever to be together, so he would make sure that life would go the way she would want it to. Becher was aware that Rita's dream would expire if Jesse James hit the bank and Iain Fulton was blasted to death, as he was sure to be.

"Taking on Jesse, Frank, the Youngers and the others will be some fight," he warned Cairew.

"We've been in tight spots before, and come out all right," Cairew looked on the bright side. "We're a good team."

"Two of us ain't much of a team," Becher cautioned, but the door opened behind them and Ike Stringer could be heard clearing his throat.

"I guess the boys have made me spokesman," he said nervously, being a better fighter than he was speaker.

Exchanging glances as they turned to face Ike, Becher and Cairew stayed quiet, but so did Stringer and Cairew was forced to ask, "Well?"

"Well, we don't reckon to know what Mel is doing, but we ain't never gone wrong since we've be'd with him, so we've decided to stick."

Both Becher and Cairew were relieved, and the former said, "Let's go back in the house; we've a whole mess of planning to do."

Inside, the men sat while Becher stood, and he was giving the basics of his scheme when Ruby entered the room with a hot drink for her father. Giving the girl a fond smile, Becher carried on talking, stopping only when Cairew interrupted by saying his name, "Mel?"

Becher paused in mid-sentence, but,

out of respect for Ruby and Zachary, Cairew didn't go on. Checking that the girl had shut the door behind her when she came into the room which meant Wheeler could hear nothing, Becher said, "There ain't nothing I wouldn't say in front of Ruby or Zachary. I guess we are all worried about Chet Wheeler, but whatever he may do against me or any of us, then Ruby ain't ever going to be a part of it."

First looking sad because of their sentiments towards her young husband, Ruby then brightened as Becher praised her, smiling at him as she sat on the arm of her father's chair, and Zachary lovingly held her there in a one-armed cuddle.

Going on to say what their campaign would be in Gallatin, Becher felt the full import of it as he heard his own voice. Not only was it daring and highly dangerous, there was, for the first time ever, nothing to be gained.

Pedro broke the solemn mood by joking. "Suits me. I was always scared of getting shot dead as I came out of a bank with a fortune in my hands."

"I reckon as how that would be better than getting gunned down while you're empty-handed," Cabel Stringer gave his opinion.

His brother agreed. "I wonder what they'll put on my tombstone — 'He died with his pockets empty'."

"They'll give you the finest epitaph you could have," Johnny Cairew told him seriously. "'He died for Mel Becher'."

11

THEY had ridden into town early that morning before the traders had opened their stores, causing curtains to twitch, women to worry, and their menfolk wondering if it would be wise to reach for firearms. Word spread quickly, reaching Iain Fulton as he walked to the bank, causing him a fear such as he had never known. Somehow, the knowledge that an outlaw gang had ridden into town, splitting up and concealing themselves so that there was no way of telling they were there, was more frightening to Fulton and the other townsfolk that the image they held of riders tearing wildly into town with guns blazing. He wondered if he should go to Rita and warn her not to venture out on the streets that day. His loyalties divided between his fiancée and the bank,

Fulton let the latter win without a struggle. But he was shaking in his shoes when he unlocked the door of the bank to allow himself and his two tellers in.

With the town on edge, the forenoon passed without incident. In Mrs Costain's parlour, Rita Martin wondered what was to happen as she listened to the wild predictions of her landlady, the only one of which that made chilling sense was that the bank was about to be robbed.

Worrying over Iain, Rita was looking out into the street just after lunch when she saw the seven men riding slowly in at the bottom end of town. Her heart missed a beat as she saw the duster-coats that she had found so frightening so short a time ago.

"Come away from the window," said a panicking Mrs Costain, pulling at the younger woman's arm as the riders dismounted and tethered their horses to a hitching rail that was just three buildings away from the bank.

But Rita refused to budge, and she picked out the man she had now accepted must be Jesse James. He was handsome enough, an extremely attractive man, but there was an off-putting coldness to his appearance, although Rita Martin was ready to concede that her mind had created this because he was the man who had murdered her father.

"Oh, good Lord," Mrs Costain moaned from what she regarded as a safe distance of some six feet back into the room. "Those men who rode in early are still here, now this lot have joined them. What is going to happen, Rita?"

Rita didn't know, but she could sense the danger in the air. She turned to her landlady, a young widow who had been prematurely aged by the sudden death of her husband. Philip Costain hadn't died by the gun, the woman had explained to Rita when she had come to the town. The Costains had intended to open a tannery in

Gallatin, but an infection Philip had picked up on the journey West had ended his life just four days after they had reached town.

"That man there, the one dusting off his hat, is Jesse James, Mrs Costain," Rita told the older woman.

Mrs Costain took the news badly. "Oh, oh, oh, my word, my word, good heavens, good heavens . . ."

Then it was Rita's turn to shudder as she saw a man walking alone from around the corner of a building, heading towards the James gang. A faint feeling swept through the girl as she recognized Mel Becher, his hard face set grimly as he strode up to the men who had now spread out, standing side by side in an arc, hands held clawlike above their holstered guns as they watched Becher's approach.

When Becher had stopped just a few yards away, Jesse James shook his head in an exaggerated show of being dumbfounded. "What are you mixing yourself into here, Mel?"

"Tired of living, Becher?" Frank James, Jesse's brother, the age gap between them made larger by a heavy moustache, asked, which had the Younger brothers and the other two men of the gang emit soft sniggers.

"This is it, Jesse, as far as you go. Just turn around and hightail it out of here," Becher said evenly.

This caused more general laughter among the gang, and Jesse James was smiling as he said, "Mighty big talk for one small man, Becher!"

"I'm not alone."

"I didn't think you were," Jesse was still smiling. "But you'll die alone here, right where you're standing now, *hombre*."

Becher's body relaxed a little, a deceptive move that Cairew or any of his men would have known was a danger sign. When Mel Becher did his gun slinging or fist-fighting, it wasn't a conscious effort, but something inside of him seemed to take over, and that something was fast, smooth, and deadly.

"If I die on this spot, James, then it will be after you are already lying dead in front of me."

Being in the presence of his men meant that Jesse James could show no trace of apprehension, let alone fear, but there was a hint of a tremor in his voice as he cautioned, "I wouldn't let getting the better of me the other day fool you, Mel."

"I've had the better of you, Jesse, from the time you rode into Quantrill's camp as a slip of a boy all those years ago." Raising his left hand, his right hovering above his holstered .45, to push his stetson a little back from his forehead, Becher went on. "Now the choice is yours: either go for your gun or mount up and ride out of town, taking Frank and these other *hombres* with you."

Flat and unequivocal, the ultimatum hung on the still air, causing the gang members, including Frank James, to move a little away from Jesse, who was tightening and slackening his jaws, the facial muscles bulging and relaxing, as a few tiny beads of sweat prickled across his brow.

Facing him, stoic as an Apache chief, Becher held James in a steady gaze, waiting for a message in Jesse's eyes to say that his right hand was on the move. In the seconds to come, there on the main street of Gallatin, the legend of Jesse James would either be enhanced or would die.

"You are a foolish man, Becher," Jesse James muttered through clenched teeth. "You'll have this street run with blood."

"Yours first," Becher half taunted him, and he saw the danger signals, the almost imperceptible twitch of Jesse's eyes, followed by a darkening of the pupils.

It was about to happen. What could only be described as a silent scream filled the street, to be suddenly replaced by a real sound — the pounding of horses' hooves.

Sheriff William McDonald, with Deputy Marshal Larren Peake came riding in at the top end of the town, heading a mass of riders. The sight of this dust-churning charge electrified the James gang, who swiftly mounted up, while Mel Becher, his confrontation with Jesse James forgotten, leapt up on to the boardwalk and squeezed himself into the shadows of a doorway as he decided what to do. His horse was quite a way off, and he'd be gunned down if he stayed in the street.

But his heroic men hadn't deserted him. Though greatly outnumbered, they stopped the ride of the lawmen, spilling two of them out of their saddles and causing the others to wheel their horses before reining them in so as to take stock of the situation.

Taking advantage of the hold-up of the posse, Becher darted round the corner of the building from whence he had come. But he wasn't the only one to use the lull caused by his gang's firing on McDonald and his men, and Becher clearly heard the order issued by Jesse James.

"The bank, men — fast."

Though the words stopped Becher's flight, he felt a great admiration for Jesse James. Outnumbered by a posse that had only been temporarily delayed by a few gunmen, he was prepared to risk hitting the bank in the short time available to him. But it was an act that Mel Becher couldn't allow him to carry out.

Coming back out on to the main street, Becher almost collided with the gang running towards the bank, with William Stiles holding the reins of all seven horses, bringing them along to the bank for a quick get-away.

As Becher fired, to be rewarded by the sight of Clell Miller clutching at his midriff and staggering, he heard Jesse curse. The whole gang stopped and turned, knowing that they had to silence Becher's gun before they could attack the bank.

Vaulting over a hitching rail, Becher dropped into the dirt, using the raised boardwalk as a flimsy protection that would last only until the James men fanned out and came to get him. Miller hadn't been badly hurt, and the fact that Stiles pulled a rifle from a scabbard on one of the horses, meant that Becher faced odds of seven to one, and the seven were all competent with a gun.

"Get him, Frank," Jesse called, and Frank James moved out a little into the street to a position where the prone Mel Becher was an easy and open target for him.

Bringing his .45 around, resigned to his own death but determined to take Frank James with him, Becher heard a wild yell from the top end of the street, followed by the mass drumming of hooves.

A large contingent of Larren Peake's men had skirted the guns of the Becher gang, and were riding down the street in Becher's direction. Abandoning the assault on the bank, the James boys and their gang members mounted up swiftly and spurred their horses towards the bottom end of town and an escape route.

With his aim accomplished, the saving of the bank and Iain Fulton, Becher no longer had any interest in the Jameses. With Peake's men riding down on his exposed position on the street, he got to his knees and ran across the road at a crouch, hearing shouts from the fast-approaching riders that told him he had been seen.

Leaping another rail, he was within feet of a dark passageway between two buildings, jumping a hay trough, when a chance bullet took him in the side, knocking him around so that he fell hard against the trough. Slowly, so slowly that he was sure he'd be shot again, Becher fell to the ground behind the trough, winded.

Lying still, he heard horses slow and

wheel about, and he knew they were looking for him.

"He's only one man," Peake shouted. "We'll pick him up on the way back. Let's get Jesse James, men."

They rode off after the Jameses. Recovering, although he could feel the blood soaking through his shirt on the left side just above the belt, and aware of intensifying pain, Becher clutched at the side of the trough to pull himself up.

Raising his head, he found himself looking into the muzzle of a rifle held by a mounted man, the only one left behind when the others had ridden off. He was elderly and unshaven, with bloodshot eyes that held a light of triumph as they looked down at Becher.

With his .45 holstered and the pain of his wound now close to intolerable, Becher had no chance of beating the rifle with a shot. But the rider was too confident. Some savage part of the man was enjoying having another human being entirely at his mercy, and it gave Becher a chance to spring into life.

His right hand moved as swiftly as a striking rattler, he reached and grasped the barrel of the rifle, tugging hard so that the surprised man came tumbling out of the saddle towards him. The rider fell across the trough, his head hanging over the side nearest to Becher, who reversed the rifle and swung it club-like against the man's skull, splitting it open with an explosive crack.

With something like half of the posse still in town, the wounded Becher was desperately in need of the now riderless horse, but it shied away from him, reared, then cantered away off down the street.

In agony now, using the rifle as a crutch, Becher hurried into the dark passageway as he heard the men who had chased after Jesse James come riding back in at the bottom of Gallatin. Hobbling along, stifling groans of pain that refused to be silenced, he made his way through a littered yard to another short road that contained only a couple of buildings. One of these, some kind of warehouse, had a small wooden shed built close by, and by squeezing into the gap between the large and the small building, Becher was able, with difficulty, to drop to the ground and roll in under the warehouse.

Lying there, he struggled out of his coat, tore the sleeves out of it, knotted them together, then tied them around his waist to cover the wound. Whether or not this served any physical purpose, Becher didn't know, but it made him feel better mentally.

Exhausted by his efforts, he lay back in the dust, hearing rats or some other small creatures scampering away from him into the deeper shadows farther under the building, as he wondered what was happening at the top end of town where he had left his men.

It was as well that, in his present condition, Becher had no knowledge of that part of town, where Peake rode up to McDonald to complain, "The Jameses got away."

Nodding as if that was what he had expected, the sheriff walked to where a body had draped itself over a water-butt that lay on its side. Reaching to entwine his fingers in the long hair of the corpse, McDonald pulled the head up to look at the face of the dead man. He allowed the head to drop back down.

"Ike Stringer." He identified the body more to himself than for Peake's benefit. "One of Mel Becher's men."

"We've lost seven men in this mess." Peake was unhappy.

"Seven?" McDonald questioned, swinging his head to the deputy marshal. "I counted six!"

"Ambrose Wilson's down the street apiece with his head stoved in. There's one of 'em passed us, McDonald."

The sheriff stayed quiet and thoughtful. The man Peake was talking about could only be Mel Becher. The whole thing was a mystery to McDonald. Those townsfolk who had been courageous enough to peek out at what was taking place in their town, had all been adamant that there had been no joint effort to rob the bank by the two gangs but, to the contrary, there had been a confrontation between Jesse James and Mel Becher. He didn't know what to make of it.

With Peake at his side, McDonald turned a corner to find a man lying face down on the ground. There wasn't that usual flat look that a dead body has, and the sheriff held his rifle at the ready as he turned the man on to his back with his foot. Pedro looked up at him and laughed his screechy laugh, but the laugh turned to a gurgling of blood in the Mexican's throat, to then become the death rattle. Though both lawmen stood transfixed by the sight of a laughing man dying in front of them, both were more than a little shaken as they walked on.

"I sure got some answering to do

when I get back," Larren Peake said morosely as he and McDonald walked into the sheriff's office. "Seven men dead, and not a thing to show for it. I had a bad feeling about this business all along, McDonald."

It had been a bad day for the sheriff, too, and he didn't want to prolong the misery by arguing with Peake, but he felt he had to put the man straight. You didn't have to come here, Peake, and things would have been mighty different if we'd come into town easy like, the way I wanted to."

"That don't alter things for me, McDonald, no matter what griping you do. Those two dead hombres out there — they ain't nothing important?"

"Just guns," McDonald admitted; "they come fifty to the dollar."

The sheriff had coffee going now, and Peake placed both hands around a mug as he drank, his cross-eyes reflecting his misery. Looking at the deputy marshal, still unable to like him, but feeling that he owed the man something for the assistance he had given, McDonald made what was part suggestion, part offer.

"If you hang around for a spell, Peake, I reckons as how we could share bringing Mel Becher in."

Interested, Peake thought it over, then shook his head to show that he was dismissing the idea. "No good, McDonald. I can't hold fourteen men here just to get Becher, despite the price on his head."

"Thirteen men," McDonald reminded Peake, seeing the unsavoury face darken. "You don't need your men. Send them on ahead and you and me can take Becher together."

Getting to his feet, Peake went to the window and looked down the street to where his man with the broken skull still lay spraddled over a hay trough. Becher was down there somewhere, he was sure of that.

"What's your plan, McDonald?"

The sheriff stood to open a cupboard and take out a box of rifle shells. "Me and my two deputies will start scouring the town for him now."

"That ain't much of a promise, Sheriff." A disgusted Peake began to gather up his rifle and shells, preparing to leave.

"It don't just rely on my finding him tonight," McDonald announced. "I know that I can pick him up any time I want to, Peake."

"You've got your hooks into one of his gang?" Peake enquired.

"Not exactly, but as good as, if not better," the sheriff replied confidently but enigmatically.

"Then I reckon as how I'll join you." Peake bared his yellow and black teeth in a grin of expectation.

12

IT was dark when Becher ventured out from under the building, by which time he was so cold that he regretted having ripped up his coat earlier. The sleeves of the coat were now stuck with blood to his shirt, which in turn adhered stiffly to the flesh of his side. Oddly, though the bullet wound was still painful, his whole body ached so much as he clambered out of his hiding place, that it took his mind off the injury.

When he did gain his feet he had to remain propped up against the wall of the small shed for a while, until his head stopped swimming and his legs not only gained strength, but agreed to do what he wanted of them.

Moving a tentative step at a time, he made his way towards the dark passageway through which he had escaped from the street. Becher could only come up with one plan, which was to steal a horse and ride out to Zachary's place. He was concerned for his men, too, Cairew in particular. There had been a lot of shooting up their end of town.

As he was about to start into the passageway, the sound of footfalls had him pull back, concealing his body behind the building while being able to peer around the corner. On the street was a man holding a lamp up high so that he could look into the passageway. The yellow glow lit a deputy badge pinned to the man's coat. It was one of McDonald's oldsters.

The deputy sheriff muttered something to himself, taking a small step into the passageway, lifting the lamp higher. Right hand going to his gun, ready to slide it from the holster, Becher hoped that the old lawman wouldn't make it necessary to silence him. Though he shrank from hurting the old fellow, his desperate situation meant that he would have to if there was no alternative.

There was a battle going on in the old deputy's head. Part of him wanted to check out the passageway. McDonald had ordered him to search thoroughly for Becher, and he wanted to do what was expected of him, but a wiser section of himself advised against foolishly risking life and limb. It was this section of his personality that won, and he grunted a couple of times to satisfy himself that there was no one there, then went back out onto the street and walked away.

Giving the old man time to be safely distant, Becher started off down the passageway, but a new sound had him freeze and flatten himself against the wall. It was voices; subdued voices, women's voices, and they were out there on the street, close to the end of the passageway.

He could see the two silhouettes at the end of the passageway now, too small to represent any threat personally, but a scream from either of them would be his undoing. He slowed his breathing and waited.

"He must be around here somewhere; it is where I lost sight of him," a female voice said anxiously.

"Frankly," he heard another woman say, "I think you are being silly, my dear."

"Believe me I am not, Mrs Costain," the first speaker protested, and Becher gave an involuntary start as he thought he recognized the voice of Rita Martin.

"The streets at night are no place for two women alone," the other female argued.

"You can go home," the voice he was now positive was Rita's said.

"And leave you alone, my dear! What on earth do you take me for? You're not thinking of venturing into that alley, are you?"

This had been asked fearfully, and received the answer, "I wish I was brave enough to do so. I'm going to risk calling."

"You can't do that." The other

woman was alarmed.

Rita, as he now knew it was, gave a little giggle. "Can't I? Just watch me." Then she put her head and shoulders into the passageway and called guardedly, "Mel Becher."

He let her call a second time before answering, the hoarseness of his voice surprising him.

They came hurrying along to him, sensing more than seeing that he was hurt when they got to him.

"Come on," Rita urged him. "Put an arm around each of our shoulders and we'll help you along."

Becher asked, "Where are you taking me?"

"To my house," Adele Costain told him firmly.

"That might get you into a lot of trouble," he husked at her.

"According to Miss Martin you are worth it," the woman told him. "Now come on, do as she says and lean on us."

He did, and they made their staggering

way along the passageway together, and he felt an immense gratitude rising in him, despite the pain of his side. Then he was thrilled because Rita Martin had put herself to a lot of trouble and risk to help him. He wanted to voice his thanks, but found himself in too much agony to say anything.

★ ★ ★

The atmosphere in the Waugh house was dismal. Zachary sat at the table, looking with sympathy at a grieving Cabel Stringer who paced up and down as he struggled to come to terms with the loss of a brother. Johnny Cairew stood anxiously at the open door, staring along the road to Gallatin as if trying to will Mel Becher to appear riding towards him. Ruby, an empty plate in her hands, came from the back room she shared with her husband, her pretty face unhappy.

"How is he?" Zachary asked, out of

love for his daughter and not interest in her husband.

"He's just about well again now, Father, although his head's still sore." She managed a wan smile. "Nothing else happened?"

"Nope," Zachary told her, then called over to Cairew. "How do you see it, Johnny?"

Without turning his head their way, Cairew spoke his thoughts. "If Mel was alive and free, he'd be back here by now!"

"You don't think . . . " Ruby began, her meaning plain.

Cairew didn't spare her, because that was his direct approach to everything. "We caught it from McDonald's men when they rode in, but Mel was in the thick of it down further. He had the Jameses at him, as well."

"Never write off Mel Becher," Zachary said, in the hope of boosting his own spirits as well as theirs.

"What will you do now?" Ruby asked Cairew.

The outlaw gave her question considerable thought before replying. "I'll give Mel until an hour before dawn, if he's not here then, we'll have to move on." He looked over at the distraught Stringer. "Will you be riding with me, Cabel?"

Stringer stopped his pacing, to stand with his head down, his voice no more than a murmur. "There ain't nothing else for me to do — but it's gonna be mighty odd without Ike."

"It's been a bad time," Zachary lamented. "A terrible time."

"My Chet didn't have nothing to do with any of it," Ruby put in defensively.

"Nobody's saying he did, child," her father said, mustering a weak smile for his daughter, and Cairew threw her a comforting look that said he agreed with Zachary.

Closing the door, Cairew came into the room, swung a chair round and sat backwards on it, his arms lying on the back, chin resting on them as he observed, "This is one of those times in life when everything changes, Zach."

Zachary nodded a sad head. "And I don't like it, Johnny."

"None of us do," Cairew concurred, "but I'll feel one hell of a lot better if Mel Becher comes walking in that door in the next few hours."

★ ★ ★

Obviously on edge, she avoided looking at Becher as she came into the room where he sat, his wound cleaned and bandaged, and wearing a shirt that had belonged to the late Philip Costain. This was the first time he had seen Rita since she and the other woman had helped him in through the door of the house. Needing to take his shirt off, Adele Costain had considered it indecent for a young single girl like Rita to be around, and had treated Becher alone. Though she had the appearance of a temperance church-goer, Mrs Costain was a woman of

180

the world, and she had given him a slug of whiskey that had fully revived him. Now, after a few short hours, he was fit enough to leave.

"You feeling better?" Rita asked him awkwardly.

"I'm fine," he told her. "Thanks for what you did — coming out to look for me, bringing me here."

Embarrassingly shrugging off his thanks, she walked over to him, as lovely as ever, her black hair making her more attractive because it tumbled loosely, ungroomed for some hours. Rita's face was very serious as she looked deeply into his eyes.

"You did it for me, didn't you," she said as a statement rather than a question.

Knowing what she meant, he was tempted to plead ignorance, but that would be a pointless ploy where an intelligent girl like her was concerned. She knew that it was for her that he had protected the bank, and there was no point in denying it. But she saved him from answering by carrying on talking herself.

"I thought you would look on me as some sort of stupid female — what with me trying to shoot you. I'm so ashamed of that."

"You were mad at Jesse James because of your father," Becher excused her. "But you could do me a big favour."

"What's that?" Rita had asked the question with an intensity that warned him she could be looking for something profound from him; such as a permanent relationship. He began to discipline himself to avoid giving her anything to seize on.

"I was going to ask you," he drawled easily, "not to try to brace Jesse James all alone."

Face blushing a deep red, she told him, "I've got over that childishness. I saw James here in town, and just the look of him terrified me. I know how lucky I was to try that stupid trick on you by mistake, and not him."

"Good; so you'll not put yourself at risk any more," he grinned, worried about what to say next, how to keep small talk going, but he was saved by the return to the room of Adele Costain.

"You'd better think of moving out," the older woman advised Becher. "Sheriff McDonald won't disturb the townsfolk at night, but as soon as it's daylight he'll be searching every house for you, I'm sure of that."

This made good sense, and Becher told her he was leaving. Getting out of town would mean him stealing a horse, as he would never find his own mount now. They asked where he would go, and, aware that he could trust them totally, he explained about Zachary Waugh's place and how he would first go there to collect the members of his gang, assuming that they were alive — the possibility that they wouldn't be having tortured him in recent hours.

There was a poignancy entering

into their relationship then, a bitter sweetness that became more acute as the time for him to leave drew nearer. The generous, caring Adele Costain had found him a coat as protection against the night air, but her husband hadn't Becher's deep chest and breadth of shoulder, so she had cut the garment down the back and sewed a piece in so that it fitted.

"You look like a hobo," she laughed self-consciously, trying to excuse what she regarded as her poor work, but Becher took her hand for a moment, holding it until she, a slight flush on her cheeks, left with the intention of packing him food for what was really a short journey.

When the old woman was out of the room, Rita said to him, "Where do I go from here?"

"Marriage to a successful bank executive," he suggested. "A nice home, children, and a long and happy life."

Acknowledging this with a little nod of her head, Rita asked, "And what of you?"

"Depends," Becher shrugged.

"On what?" she asked avidly.

"On whether my men are still alive."

"If they are, will you go on living as you always have?"

There was danger in her question, he recognized that. If he told her that his intention was to continue as an outlaw, then everything between them would end there. He couldn't be sure what made him give the answer he did — whether it was because he had been for some time considering changing his life, or because he couldn't bear to break with her completely.

Whatever; he told her, "I'm thinking about leaving that sort of life."

Mrs Costain's footsteps could be heard approaching from the kitchen, and Rita moved close to him, urgency in her whisper. "What was the name of your friend with the house outside of town?"

185

"Waugh," he told her. "Zachary Waugh."

"I'll find it," she told him, her tone soft but confident. "Wait for me. I'll meet you there tomorrow."

Becher wanted to protest, to talk her out of it by stressing how she had everything that she needed here in town. Most important of all was the stability that meant so much to women. To leave Gallatin and follow him would mean that she probably would never again know security. There was so much he had to tell her, so many reasons why she shouldn't follow the course she planned — a course built on nothing but physical attraction.

Was that last bit true, he wondered as Adele Costain came smilingly back into the room, carrying a package of food for him. The magnetism between Rita and himself seemed to have roots into something deeper than a superficial feeling.

All he wanted to say remained unsaid as the two women saw him to the door, checking the street outside first to make sure that it was deserted. Then he was outside and the door closed quietly behind him. This was the real world, the world of hardship, danger, and death that he knew so well. Now he was back into it, merely by taking one step out over a threshold, his time with Rita, though it had ended only minutes ago, was now nothing but a vague and distant dream.

Keeping close to the shadows of the buildings, he made his light-footed way to where he seemed to remember a livery was located. Once he had a horse beneath him he would ride out of this town and into reality.

13

SHAKING him enthusiastically by the hand, refusing to stop, determined not to let go, Zachary Waugh used his other hand to bang out a welcome on Mel Becher's back.

"You ornery crittur, Mel. Dang it, I knew they couldn't get you," the older man crowed. "Come on, set yourself at the table. I'll get that gal of mine out of bed to get you some vittles."

Wanting to stop his friend, his stomach well satisfied by the food Adele Costain had supplied, which he had eaten along the trail, Becher knew it would hurt Zachary to do so. But he was in no hurry. He could sit and toy with the food, as it would soon be dawn, and he couldn't leave here until nightfall. It would be risky to do otherwise in the circumstances. He wasn't surprised that his boys weren't here. They would have thought it safer to move on. They would, he knew, be waiting at Hatton's Peak for him.

Coming back, Zachary, grinning in delight, sat across the table from Becher, eager to ask many things, but aware that Becher had questions of his own.

"What happened to the boys, Zach?" he asked, and felt a coldness creeping through him as the grin changed into a grimace of emotional pain.

"Cairew?" he asked sharply, fearing the worst.

Waving an arm to reassure his friend, Zachary said, "No, Johnny's fine. All that's worrying him is you, Mel. He said you'd know where to find him if you turned up. Hatton's Peak, I reckons."

"That's right," a relieved Becher told him. "What about the others?"

"Cabel Stringer's OK, Mel," Zachary told him the bad news indirectly.

"Ike and Pedro?" he said, hurt more than he thought possible.

"Sorry, Mel," Zachary nodded, as Ruby came hurrying into the room, an old coat on over her nightclothes.

Rushing to Becher, the girl threw her arms around him, hugging him, kissing his face. "Oh, Mel. I thought that they'd killed you!"

"I'm not that easy to get rid of, Ruby." He found that he could smile as he returned her embrace, moved by her feelings for him. Behind her in the doorway she had come through, stood Chet Wheeler, looking out into the room as he tucked his shirt-tails into his trousers.

With Ruby still hugging him, Becher exchanged anxious glances, but then Wheeler came striding across to the table, his right hand stretched out to Becher. "I'm right pleased to see you back, Becher. No hard feelings?"

"None at all."

Standing, Becher shook the boy's hand, while Ruby still held on to his arm, desperate to retain contact, but she was smiling happily between her husband and Becher. Chet Wheeler had come of age, and even Zachary had lost the usual hardness from his eyes as he looked at his son-in-law.

"I reckon as how you two youngsters ought to leave Mel alone to eat," Zachary told Ruby and Chet, then addressed Becher. "I'll allow you could use some shut-eye, too, Mel?"

Admitting he would welcome sleep, Becher went to his bed after eating. Though his side was sore it wasn't giving any serious trouble, and he was surprised to find when lying down how exhausted he was. The sleep he enjoyed was a deep one, but he was awake at noon, his mind quickly filling with the problems that he faced. With Ike and Pedro dead, and assuming that Cabel Stringer stayed with him, they would either need to recruit new members for the gang, or curtail the scale of their robberies. Also in his head was a reluctance to go back to the old life. His friendship with Cairew, which went back over many years, was important to him, but he felt that it could continue in a more peaceful, lawful way of life.

Then there was what Rita had said in what seemed a solemn promise. Yet he doubted that her resolve would stand daylight and the realization of what she had said she would take on. When she met her fiancé that day, a reliable, dependable, law-abiding young man, she would surely count her blessings and change her mind as a consequence.

What should have taken priority over his thoughts, who should have been uppermost in his mind — Sheriff McDonald — came into his head then. Being an old friend of Zachary, McDonald, even if he suspected that Becher was holed up here, would not come riding in, but would patiently wait for the time that Mel Becher went riding out. The advantage that Becher held was that McDonald wouldn't know which trail he would take, and didn't have the manpower to cover every exit track from the Waugh homestead.

A secondary worry for Becher were the men riding with McDonald the previous day. They might well still be around, but after some contemplation, he doubted it. With half of his gang dead — which reminded him that he must send Ike Stringer's mother in Missouri money, poor recompense for the loss of a son, but all he could do — those men were probably on the trail of the James boys and the Youngers by now.

Getting up, he walked out into the sunshine. With Zachary nowhere to be seen, Becher walked to a rain-barrel at the side of the house, pulled off his shirt, and washed himself thoroughly, though avoiding wetting the bandage Adele Costain had so skilfully applied.

Dressed again and feeling fresher, he walked over to the corral, where he leaned on the rail, enjoying the sunshine, attempting to shape the immediate future for himself. He found it easier to think out here in the fresh air, and the things that had looked so bad to him, lightened in the brightness of the afternoon.

Unusually for him, a shadow alerted him that someone was near, instead of his instinct and natural responses warning him of a presence. Brushing his holstered gun with his right hand, ready for whatever might be coming, he swung swiftly to face the shadow, and found himself looking at an unsmiling Ruby.

"Where's your father?" he asked, relaxing again, turning to rest his arms back on the rail.

"Gone over to the Melstock place to get some smithy work done," Ruby told him, her voice flat and moody. "He said to tell you he'll be back before nightfall."

This made Becher smile. Zachary was scared he'd ride out on him without an *adios*. Many times the old man had told him how lonely and empty his homestead was when he and his gang weren't around. It could be said that Zach thought of him as a son, that was if you didn't know that the old man's intention had been to have him as a son-in-law. Same thing, in a way, Becher mused now.

"You leaving tonight, Mel?"

Without facing the girl, he nodded. "Yep."

Her hand reached out to touch his left forearm, the nearest one to her, then travelled up to squeeze his bicep before moving over his shoulders. Then Ruby was close, clutching him to her, as she begged, "Take me with you."

Becher tried to move away, but she held on to him staying close, and he was drastically aware of the problems her behaviour could bring. "Where's Wheeler?"

"In the house," she pouted. "But I don't care no more."

Becher tried to free himself from her embrace. "I do," he told her, and he did, because the house wasn't far away, it had windows, and Chet Wheeler had eyes. From that distance, what was a one-sided and unwelcome embrace would look like something very different.

"I knew when you came back, when Daddy got me from my bed early this morning," she was talking rapidly. "I knew then, Mel, what you meant to me, what you mean to me."

"You're married to that boy down there," he reminded her.

"That was a mistake," she countered, pulling him closer.

"What do you think this would do to your father, Ruby?" He tried to make her see sense. "Think of him."

"I've thought of my father all of my life, and now I'm going with you, Mel."

Becher cast his eyes about for something to save him. Zachary Waugh riding over the horizon would have been a welcome sight, but the range was deserted. There was only the house, and its watching eyes.

"You can't come with me, Ruby, it don't make sense!"

"Why not?" the girl challenged him.

"I can cook and look after you, and I can shoot as good as any man."

Pulling her hands from where they clutched at his shoulders, he held her at arm's length, and hated himself when he saw her face collapse into misery as he told her the truth. "I don't want you with me, Ruby."

The girl began to cry and, against his better judgement, he put his arm round her to comfort her. Burying her face against his chest, Ruby sobbed and he could feel her body shaking. Looking unseeingly and unhappily over her head, his eyes suddenly snapped into focus as they saw movement at the back of the house. Chet Wheeler, mounted on a fast horse, galloped away in the direction of Gallatin, going so fast that both him and his mount were soon nothing more than a small, moving balloon of dust.

This was what Becher had dreaded from the moment Ruby had touched him. Chet Wheeler, a sulky, untrustworthy fellow at the best of times, must

197

now consider himself to be a wronged husband, and he would be dangerous as a consequence. When McDonald learned from the boy that Becher was here, and that Zachary Waugh was away from home, the sheriff wouldn't hesitate to come for him.

He had to get away. Without a word, Becher thrust Ruby roughly from him and ran across to the lean-to at the back of the house, where Zachary had left his horse after taking care of it when he got back. Hearing the shouting Ruby running behind him, he took no notice, but grabbed the saddle, threw it on to the startled horse, buckled the cinch, then reached for the bit and reins.

As Ruby ran into the lean-to, Becher was riding out, so fast that she almost collided with his horse, and he saw the fright on the girl's face as he went charging by.

★ ★ ★

Chet Wheeler hadn't got far from the house when he had to rein in his horse suddenly as McDonald spurred his horse out from one side of the track to confront him, while another man did the same from the other side.

"In kinda a hurry, son," the sheriff said, blinking through the dust kicked up by Wheeler's horse as it slid to a sudden halt.

"I was coming for you, Sheriff," Chet Wheeler said, then blurted out the whole story of Becher being at the Waugh place, and Zachary being away, leaving out only his motive — mention of seeing his wife in the arms of Mel Becher.

"Than we'd best ride along there," McDonald said, but the other man held up a hand to stop him.

"What's the trouble, Peake?" the sheriff enquired.

Not answering him, Peake turned his cross-eyes on to the boy. "Does Becher know you left?"

"Reckon he see'd me," Chet nodded.

"Reckon as how he see'd me ride out."

At this, Larren Peake wheeled his horse, riding slowly off at an angle to the Waugh homestead, causing McDonald to call after him, "Where you going, Peake?"

"To hit the high ground," the deputy marshal told him, riding on.

Pausing for a moment, the sheriff saw the logic in this, and spurred his horse to go in the wake of Peake, signalling to Wheeler to follow them.

★ ★ ★

Riding fast, Becher was confident that he could get away long before Wheeler had chance to contact the sheriff and bring him to Zachary's place. The trick was not to use the Gallatin road, along which the dedicated McDonald was sure to come. That was no problem, for Becher had neither a reason or a desire to go to the town. His aim was to reach Hatton's Peak, where Johnny

Cairew and a much-needed sense of proportion would be waiting for him. He regretted not seeing Zachary before he left, but the actions of the old man's daughter had given him no option.

Thinking of the disturbed girl had him turn his head, and his nerves jangled as he saw dust following him. There was only one rider, but that could well be the intrepid Will McDonald. Backing his horse between two huge boulders, Becher was confident that he had the time to identify the rider, then ride on before he could catch up with him.

Less than five minutes later he made the grim discovery that it was Ruby following him. Born and bred on the range, the girl had lost no time in saddling up and hitting the trail behind him.

This altered his plans. Outriding the girl was no solution, for eventually, sooner or later, probably sooner, she would catch up with him. What he had to do was throw her off his trail.

He needed to get going straight, put as much distance between this place and himself as quickly as possible. Ruby would know this, and wouldn't expect him to waste time in making a detour. This was what he had to do: ride in a sweeping arc, letting her go straight, then crossing the trail she had left and heading for Hatton's Peak along a less direct route than this one.

Bringing the horse out from behind the boulders, he rode off at a tangent, keeping his horse at a canter so as not to kick up dust to alert the girl.

Riding steadily for an hour, looking over his shoulder at regular intervals, he was confident that Ruby wasn't behind. Satisfied that he had shaken her off, he increased the pace of the horse, and was about to make one final check of the trail behind him when the animal under him reacted to something ahead, reared up.

Regaining control of the horse, Becher rode round a bend into a canyon to find his way blocked. Sitting side by side on horses, each holding a rifle on him, were Sheriff McDonald and Chet Wheeler, although the boy's rifle wavered and his face showed fear.

"End of the trail for you I'd say, Becher!" McDonald told him, his face grim.

That might have been the lawman's opinion, but it wasn't Becher's. Feeling the old familiar, comforting response throughout his body, he knew what he had to do: spur the horse forward while slipping off its back over its rump. Wheeler wasn't a problem, Becher could cut him down easily, and the sheriff would first have to contend with the horse coming at him. That would be enough of a diversion for Becher to draw and blast the lawman out of the saddle.

Putting the plan into action, Becher hit the sides of his horse hard with his spurs. The animal leapt forwards as he went wide-legged over the back, drawing his .45 as he hit the ground, hearing the grunt of alarm come from

McDonald as the charging horse caused his own mount to shy.

As if in slow motion, the whole scene was laid out clearly for Becher. McDonald's horse was rampant, temporarily protecting the sheriff from Becher, who fired a shot that took the side of Chet Wheeler's head away.

Watching the boy topple sideways, dead long before he hit the dirt, Becher moved slightly to be ready to plug the sheriff as his horse came down. It was then he saw the man standing to one side, having come out from a crevice in the rocks of the canyon. He was ugly and unshaven, the grin on his face not reaching the cross-eyes that were steady on Becher, as steady as the rifle the man held to his hip with one hand, while the other seemed to be reaching for something in the crevice.

There was still nothing to really worry Becher. McDonald's horse was back on all fours, but its rider hadn't recovered enough to bring his rifle back on to Becher, who prepared to gun down the cross-eyed man, then drop and roll, picking the sheriff off as he did so.

Tightening his finger on the trigger, he couldn't fathom why the ugly man hadn't brought his other hand in so that he could use the rifle. The out-of-line eyes were looking at death, but the man didn't seem to care. Then he jerked harder with his left hand, pulling something out of the crevice and putting it between Becher and himself.

Only just able to hold his fire, Becher saw that it was Ruby the man was using as a shield. They must have been watching and waiting, first capturing her.

McDonald had brought his rifle back to bear on Becher now, and the cross-eyed man dragged Ruby further over so that she was in a position where Becher could fire neither at the sheriff nor the ugly man without the high risk of hitting her.

A kind of paralysis gripped Becher as

hè had to accept that he was beaten. He saw triumph in the cross-eyes as the man prepared to fire the rifle one-handed from the hip, and watched the top lip lift up over long and yellow teeth. McDonald, too, was curling his finger around the trigger of his rifle, but there was no gloating on his face, but more of a melancholy expression. Waiting for the inevitable, Becher heard Ruby's half-screamed apology.

"I'm sorry, Mel!"

14

S HE felt guilty as she paid the man at the livery for the hire of the horse, for Rita Martin's plans didn't include returning the animal. After a completely sleepless night, being unable to rest after Mel Becher had crept furtively from the house, she had eaten breakfast while struggling with herself inside of her head, and it wasn't until a very short time ago that the battle within her had ceased. Not that it was really over, for there were casualties — like Iain Fulton and Adele Costain.

Yet there was no way that she could now contemplate a mundane life in a small town like Gallatin. Being the wife of a bank executive brought a lot of respect and possibly admiration, definitely envy, but that wasn't what she wanted. She had to have a life of adventure now, with uncertainty and excitement in every hour. It was the kind of life that a woman could live and enjoy if she had the right man at her side, and Mel Becher was most definitely the man for her.

In making her decision she had, for the first time ever, let herself down, first with Adele Costain and then Iain Fulton. Her landlady, who had so selflessly helped Becher, deserved the truth, but Rita had been unable to bring herself to tell her. Mrs Costain had said a cheery farewell to her, already planning the tea she would have ready for them when Rita returned from what she lied was a horse ride out of town to clear her mind, something that always worked for her back East.

"Take care," Adele Costain had cautioned. "Don't ride too far. Always keep the town in sight if you can."

Agreeing, Rita had left and gone to the bank, determined to at least hint to her fiancé that things were not going to go the way he anticipated.

Had Mel Becher been a rancher or a merchant, she told herself, but didn't know whether she could believe it, she would have had no hesitation in letting down Iain, but she would have done it lightly. There again, having seen the wildness in her when she had been ready to kill Mel Becher, he might be able to understand. Nevertheless, he would have stopped her from leaving, even by bringing the law down upon Becher.

In the bank, with Iain having fully recovered from the trauma of the previous day, and full of excited plans that included her, Rita hadn't found the courage to tell him the drastic move she was about to make, and she had left Iain believing, just like Mrs Costain, that she was taking a short, constitutional ride. To encourage this belief, Rita had left most of her belongings behind, things she had owned most of her life, but nostalgia could play no part in a new start.

The horse beneath her was made

placid with age, but still had enough verve to cover long distances if not pushed. So she chose a steady gait as she left the buildings of Gallatin behind her and headed east in the general direction in which she thought the Waugh homestead lay.

A few miles out of town she saw a homesteader off to her left, fighting a plough pulled by a powerful mule, and she angled off the road to reach him, asking the way to the Waugh place.

"Keep on going thataway." The man used his head to gesture as he struggled at his task. "Make for those two peaks yonder. Head between them and you'll come upon Zach Waugh's place around ten miles farther on."

Waving her thanks as the mule dragged her informant off in a staggering run through his rutted land, Rita rode on towards the distant hills, growing tired long before the peaks the man had indicated had become a distinct sight rather than a blur. Only the thought of joining up with Mel Becher kept her going. Though she had told him that she would be riding to him, he was such a difficult man to understand that she wasn't sure if he believed her, and if so, whether he would wait until she arrived.

She had a choice now as the trail forked to become two separate tracks on different levels. The homesteader hadn't warned her of this, and Rita was undecided, halting her horse while she considered her alternatives. By aligning herself with the gap between the peaks, she felt sure that the lower trail was the one she should take. Moving off, she had only covered a short distance when the sight of horsemen coming towards her made her apprehensive.

As they grew closer, she felt her dread turn to fear. Rita had been hoping, even praying, that this could be Mel Becher coming to look for her, but there were two riders, neither of whom resembled Becher. Each led what from a distance looked to her like a laden pack-horse.

Rita Martin relaxed as the riders came closer and she saw the afternoon sun glinting off the stars that both men wore. As they drew nearer they veered a little so that they wouldn't pass close to Rita, and the rider nearest to her, a large man, no longer young, with a heavy moustache, raised his right hand, still holding the reins of his horse, to tip his stetson respectfully.

"Howdy, ma'am."

Nodding, Rita then went cold as she realized that each of the two horses led by the men was loaded with a body draped over the saddle, Seeing the direction of her gaze, the big man told her. "Don't look too closely this way, ma'am."

That was why they had skirted away from her, she realized, and the horse led by the big man moved restlessly, causing the head of the dead man over its saddle to waggle. The horrific attracts, and Rita could not pull her eyes away. Nodding to his companion, who was staring at her with crossed-eyes, the big man had them both move on, with him again touching the rim of his hat.

"Good day, ma'am."

Giving a weak smile of acknowledgement, Rita was able to take her eyes from the body as the horse walked on. Then curiosity had her look at the horse led by the cross-eyed man. This body was large, making the first one seem like that of a boy.

The cross-eyed man touched his stetson in farewell. "Ma'am."

She nodded to him as he went past her. Now she had a better view of the second body. There was something odd there that she couldn't categorize for a moment, then she realized what it was and a hand flew to her mouth in horror.

The body lay face down, and the coat it had on had been divided at the back and a material of a different colour sewn in!

Giving a little cry, Rita startled

both lawmen by wheeling her horse and sending it galloping back in the direction from which she had come. A sickness was rising in her as she rode desperately, the old horse surprised by what was being asked of it, but doing its best.

As the town of Gallatin came into view the horse had made all the effort it could manage, and it had slowed considerably. There was a parallel drop in the ill feeling and horror in Rita Martin. As they entered the main street, with the horse blowing and sweating, she realized, with a shock, that at that moment she had returned to a state of sanity that had deserted her at the time Jesse James and Mel Becher had faced each other on this very street.

Taking the horse to the livery, where the hostler gave it a worried glance before bestowing a reproachful glare on Rita for having misused the animal.

Walking back to the house of Mrs Costain, Rita slowed as she passed the bank, hoping that, if Iain was